By the Sound of the Crow

I Know You're There Sequel

Susan Allison-Dean

Published by Sea and Farm
Copyright 2014 Susan Allison-Dean

Cover Design: Tugboat Design
Interior Formatting: Tugboat Design
www.tugboatdesign.com

ISBN: 978-0-9908968-07

My Deepest Gratitude

If I could, I would find each of you who read my debut
novel and give you each a big hug.

Your support of this new endeavor has inspired me to
continue to hone the craft of writing.

Special thanks to all those who wrote reviews, rated my first
book, posted comments on Facebook and Twitter, and/or
contacted me directly.

Once again, a big thank you to Deborah at Tugboat Design
for another beautiful cover design.

To Alice Osborn, my editor and writing coach.

To the North Castle Library for allowing me to use their
quiet office to write.

To Joanne Dobson, author and writing instructor at the
Hudson Valley Writers' Center, and my fellow fiction-
writing classmates. Your support and feedback have helped
me immeasurably.

To my family and friends. What would life be without you?

To My Loving Husband

Robert

By the Sound of the Crow

Prologue

BANE

JANUARY 1996

Bane parked his Jeep on the side of the road and sat there. Slowly, he rolled himself out and trudged through the narrow sandy path overtaken by brush. He didn't seem to feel the scrapes of the branches or the thorny jabs from the rosa rugosa shrubs. When he broke free from the path, he stood and surveyed the blanket-sized patch of sand leading to the sea. He plucked a strand of dune grass and began to chew on it. He would wait here.

He sat down and allowed himself to lean back resting on both his elbows, legs outstretched. He watched the fluffy white clouds morph into shapes. A lone pelican flew by, eyeing the water for fish.

At the sound of a roar of a jet, he braced himself. It flew right over him, near enough that he could have tossed a shell at it. His eyes followed the plane that carried Jill away.

A tear dripped down the side of his face and he leaned forward to wipe it away before it reached his chin. *Another one gone*, he thought. This one was different, though. This woman touched him deeper, more intimately somehow. Was it possible for two people to feel so connected in just one week? Perhaps it was because they both shared something in common-they were both running away from something. Escaping to Triton as a way out of life's problems.

As the roar of the jet whispered away, Bane was once again left with just the sound of the waves lapping along the shoreline as he traced a heart in the sand and then stood up. He brushed the sand away from his shorts and looked down again at the heart. There was a part of him that wanted to get on the next plane to New York and straighten things out with Jill. He really hated the way things ended between them; he had a rotten feeling in his stomach.

The time that Bane spent lost out at sea made him think and confront a lot of things he was trying to avoid, especially the reason he came to Triton.

"Please, please, come home," his mother begged him on the phone this very morning. Home, back to Hawaii.

His roommate Tom had called Bane's parents when it got dark that first night Bane was lost at sea. Luckily he was found before his family took the long journey from Hawaii to Triton. Originally Bane planned to come to Triton for a three-month commitment to be a dive instructor. Three months, turned into a year, then two.

At first, Bane's mother was supportive of his adventure.

"Spread your wings a bit; see some other parts of the world. But come back soon. Hawaii is the most beautiful place," she said with her warm smile that made her eyes melt into her pudgy dark skin.

His dad said nothing, his way of saying he wasn't happy at all with Bane's decision to go to Triton. "Bane" meant long-awaited son in Hawaiian.

With his hands firmly planted in his pockets, Bane gently swept the heart away with his right foot until it was once again just one big pile of miniscule crushed coral. He couldn't help but wonder—what if he had drowned out there? How would his father react? He knew it would have broken his mother's heart. If Jill had the strength to go back and face the troubles she left at home, maybe it was time for him to do the same.

* * *

The first person he shared his decision with was the one person Bane knew would be overjoyed about it, his mother.

"Thank God!" she screamed in the phone. "Joe, Bane is coming home." Her husband sat at the kitchen table reading the local paper. There was silence in return. "He's very excited too," she reported back to her son enthusiastically.

Once he told his mother his plan, it cemented his decision. There was no turning back now. He would never break her heart. As he hung up the phone, he looked at the view outside the window of the cottage he shared with his mates. Sunny-with a gentle wind whispering through the fronds of the palm trees, as usual. The bright blue-green water of the bay shimmered in the distance. Yes, Hawaii was beautiful, but it didn't have water as crystal clear as Triton's.

He meandered over to the refrigerator, filled a glass up with cold milk, and then leaned against the counter in the galley kitchen that was way too tight for five guys to fit in all at once. The house was quiet except for the wind trying to sneak in the cracks of the windows. The welcome silence gave him time to think how he would tell his friends that he would be leaving. They had become close, like brothers, over the years.

It had been Tom's idea for them to pool their money together and get a place of their own. Living at the resort they worked at got tiring. Tom had been living on the island the longest. Bane gathered that he came from fairly wealthy family in Miami. Being the last of five kids, a mix of boys and girls, his parents seemed like they ran out of expectations for their children and allowed Tom to follow his passion, scuba diving. They came to visit him on occasion and the guys were always thrilled when they did. It meant a few nights of really good dinners out.

Max, the chap from Australia, arrived in Triton a month after Bane did. His thick curly hair and Down Under accent were a big hit with the ladies.

Max was their resident mechanic. He maintained all the boats and equipment at the resort. A real guy's guy. They were glad to have him as part of their group, especially when their cars needed fixing. Having cars repaired on an island with scarce resources was no easy feat.

Yosef from Israel really knew how to cook and had a happy-go-lucky, peaceful presence. When the guys began scouting for a fourth housemate, his name made it to the top of the list quickly. The four of them were eager to break free from always being on call at the resort. It was hard to say no to their constant needs since the resort was paying for the roof over their heads.

It started out as the four of them, each with their own rooms. Then along came Mason.

Mason always claimed to originally hail from California. But Bane knew different. California was actually the last place Mason was from before he came to Triton. Originally from the Midwest, Mason was born to an unwed teen mother who gave motherhood a half-hearted attempt. It wasn't long before he was being passed around in foster homes. By the time he was fifteen, he had lived in over a dozen places and knew he was coming to the age where it was highly unlikely he would ever find somewhere to really call home.

It was the big storm of 1994, just after his seventeenth birthday, that propelled him to take a chance. Mason was shoveling three feet of snow, as more barreled down, his toes all frozen popsicles. He decided then and there—no more of this. After the storm subsided and the sun broke out, Mason packed a duffle bag, headed for the highway and hitched a ride going west.

The old-timers in the diner always talked about California. "I should have moved there, sunny every day," Mason heard them say. That's where he would go, goodbye snow.

It took four different truckers to get him to sunny California. The final one dropped him off at Venice Beach.

"You should fit in here, son," the old codger of a driver told him. There were Jesus pictures, crosses and biblical sayings tucked all around the inside of his cab. Mason took it as a sign that his luck might be turning. He got out of the front cab and stepped into the promised sun.

The truck driver was right. Mason did fit in the Venice Beach scene, at least for a while. The quirky group of people from all over didn't ask a lot of questions. It was easy for him to blend in. With only a few dollars to his name he took residence on a park bench using his sweatshirt as a pillow. The outdoor shower faucets on the boardwalk, which were meant for people to rinse sand off, allowed him to shower daily. He learned the gift of gab, especially with the girls on the beach. They generously shared the healthy food that filled their coolers.

The surfers who owned the waters along the beach mesmerized Mason. He knew how to swim thanks to one of his foster families who insisted he learn. After watching their moves, he eventually got brave enough to talk with them.

"Those were some really cool moves." Mason would toss to a lone surfer.

"Thanks, man." Or something along those lines was the most they would typically say in return. Until one day, a lanky guy only a little taller than Mason, and just a few years older said, "Do you want to try it?"

"Try it? Hell yeah!" he exclaimed.

Mason was a natural at surfing. He was instantly hooked. For the first time in his life, he felt like he belonged on the planet. Being in sync with the natural rhythm of the ocean gave him a high that he had never experienced.

It wasn't long before his natural abilities were noticed and he got to know some of the established regulars catching the waves. He was keenly aware of the curious looks coming from the beach. Mason took advantage of their longing and started offering surf lessons. It didn't pay enough for him to get a room, but he ate at the local eateries and upgraded his surfboard from the second hand one an older surfer gave him. Mason had finally found a home: the sea.

Rummaging through the trash one night, looking for recycled cans to return, Mason found himself a recent copy of *Dive* magazine. He rolled it up and tucked it in his back pocket. Under the light of a lamppost, he leafed through it. Other than sharks, which they all kept an eye out for, he didn't give much thought to what lived below him as he buoyed on his surfboard waiting for the next perfect wave. Apparently there was a lot, and he was intrigued.

As he flipped to the last couple of pages, he noticed a want ad: "All inclusive resort on Triton Island looking for help: dive instructors, boat captains, waiters, housekeeping, front desk clerks and more. Contact us for details." Mason didn't bother contacting them. He increased his surfing lessons until he had stockpiled enough money for a ticket to the island. How could they say no to him for a job if he were already there?

* * *

One by one, Bane told his housemates that he would be

leaving the island, moving back to Hawaii.

Tom was bummed but he understood.

Max, as expected, grabbed his hand firmly and slapped his shoulder as he said, "Best of luck to ya, mate. We'll miss ya around here."

Yosef subdued his joy, as he would no longer have to share his room with Mason.

Telling Mason would be the hardest. Bane procrastinated until he could no longer avoid it. He called Mason and made arrangements to meet for lunch at the Harbor Side Café.

* * *

Mason was at a table sipping an ice tea when Bane arrived. Bane ordered the same and his usual, conch salad roll with fries. He was sure going to miss conch salad when he got back to Hawaii. They chatted casually about Mason's surf group that morning until the waitress served their meals. Bane let Mason get a few bites in before he shared the news.

"What about all the plans we were making? What about owning our own dive company?" Mason said with his fork firmly clenched in his hand.

"I'm sorry, Mason, I really am. I need to do this; I need to go back home. Why don't you come with me? We can start a dive company in Hawaii." Bane pushed his plate away, no longer hungry.

"Easy for you to say," Mason stood up, grabbed the napkin from his lap, threw it on the table and stormed out of the restaurant.

Bane held his head in his hands as he gazed out over the railing onto the harbor. *That was a stupid thing to say*, he thought. Bane knew it wouldn't be easy for Mason to return to the States. He got on the island with a fake driver's license he had made in California before Triton required a passport for entry. Mason had no idea where his original birth certificate was and had no money, nor contacts, to find it. The two of them had dreamed of creating a business of their own on the island. For Bane, it was always more of a dream. For Mason, apparently, it was a reality. He wished Mason had taken the news as easily as the others. Why did it seem like he was always leaving people disappointed?

"Check?" Eloise asked softly as she gathered the plates on the table.

"Yeah, sorry." Bane saw she had been watching their table during their confrontation. He reached in his pocket for his wallet. It was time to go and start packing. He had a bigger problem to tackle.

The sun may light the day, but the moon never disappears.

2012

Chapter 1

JILL

My bed begged me to get back in. My boisterous family, however, reminded me that I couldn't without having to explain why. Fall always brought a sense of dread, but this year, for some reason, more so. I felt surrounded by death and doom. The only way out was an option I contemplated years ago. I decided against that back then. *No, I will soldier on.*

The creaky wooden stairs announced my awakening: I've officially joined the family.

"Bye, Mom," Sarah shouted but didn't look at me as she ran out the front door. Her naturally wavy long, thick hair flew flat as a piece of paper behind her.

"But, the bus won't be coming for another fifteen minutes." I tried to hold her back. The door slammed. I paused at the bottom step. The rush of water through the pipes told me where my husband was and confirmed what I knew; Sarah painted her face with makeup while he was taking care of business, hoping they'd miss each other.

I found Amanda slurping up the last of her granola cereal, while she stared at her homework propped up on the sugar bowl.

"Good morning, honey," I said as I poured Goddess Kaffeina into my favorite handmade mug. "Mom" chiseled in the side surrounded by a heart. "Test today?"

"Yeah," Amanda confirmed. "Math."

"Do you want me to quiz you?" I offered. Although I wasn't sure if I even know how to do math the way they do it today.

"No, that's okay." She filed her papers in her book bag by the door and headed upstairs.

I tightened my robe but still felt the frigid air creeping into my bones. Knowing Luke would say something, I turned the heat up.

As soon as the baseboard heat started to crackle, Luke shouted from upstairs, "It's too early to turn the heat on! It's not even November yet." He's so predictable.

While I am thankful that he brings the left side of the brain to the table with his accounting skills, sometimes it gets annoying. Must we account for every penny?

Fall announced its presence loudly the weekend before when the temperature dipped to 39 degrees. Apples in crates now lined the farmer's market stands: Golden Delicious, Honey Crisp, and McIntosh. Their sweet scent replaced the rich aroma of basil and tomatoes. Pumpkins were beginning to arrive, ready to be carved into funny faces.

I gazed out of the windows that need to be washed. The lush green leaves on the trees were starting to turn gold. It's always the maples that start the metamorphosis. Bright yellow, burnt orange, and merlot mums had begun replacing the containers in front of the homes in our neighborhood that were overflowing with purple petunias, multi-color coleus, and red geraniums all summer. I always felt best during the summer surrounded by all the colors and textures and the generous days of sunlight. I had already started to mourn their loss.

The change of seasons brought excitement for the kids. There were new things to do; football games, cheerleading, and biking is more pleasurable. Even Peaches enjoyed walking further in the cooler temps. But as the days dimmed, I was reminded that we were heading down that path again, the one with no exit, no way out. I was going to be forced to relive the night of the accident and all its fatal consequences. For sixteen years those memories stayed buried under my busyness; getting married, moving, decorating and restoring an old farmhouse, raising two little girls, switching jobs.

Life had begun to slow down, almost shift into autopilot. The old memories took advantage of the freed up space in my brain, creeping out of the graveyard like Halloween zombies.

I was reminded, yet again, over and over that I was forewarned. Someone, was it God, a guardian angel, or my own subconscious, tried to tell me not to volunteer to work that extra shift at the hospital. It wasn't like I heard a voice. No, it was more like an internal hint or just a sense of knowing that came from deep inside. I guess that's what they call a gut feeling.

If nothing else, I've learned to listen to the inner wisdom when I feel it now. *Don't stop for milk tonight. Get it tomorrow.* Who knows what I may have avoided by heading to that suggestion. *Make a stuffed-roast chicken for dinner.* I did, and later found out that Luke had a really bad day. Having his favorite dinner waiting for him when he got home really cheered him up.

"Sure you don't want to come?" Luke interrupted my thoughts as he poured a cup of coffee in his travel mug, his gym bag slung over his shoulder. *I should join him at the gym*, I thought. God knows I could stand to lose a few pounds too. But I was in no mood to rush out the door that day.

Completely unaware that he had a severe case of bedhead made my heart warm. *He's looking good*, I thought. I didn't dare tell him that. He probably would have stopped working out. He only had maybe another ten pounds and he'd be in the right weight range for a guy six foot two.

"No, thanks, maybe tomorrow." Luke kissed me on the cheek; I reached up and smoothed down his hair.

"Are you okay?"

"Fine." I smiled. Our eyes lingered, he touched my cheek with his big warm hand before he headed out. I wanted to melt. Cry. Say, *I can't get Samantha out of my head.* "You go get that workout in. You're almost at your goal weight!"

Amanda thundered into the kitchen and opened the refrigerator door. It was hard to believe in one more year my baby would be going to high school. Sarah was already there as a sophomore.

"Mom, Sarah took my lunch!" Amanda cried as she

burrowed through the fridge.

"Maybe it was an accident." I tried to calm her, but I had a feeling the exchange was deliberate. There was only enough turkey left for one sandwich so someone had to settle for peanut butter and jelly. The girls battled for the turkey the night before with a two out of three game of rock, scissors, paper. Amanda won. However, the day before she borrowed Sarah's favorite blue cardigan sweater without asking. They were either the best of friends or the worst of enemies, those two. Friends of mine who have sisters tell me that's just the way it is, especially if they are close in age. I never got the chance to experience the sister relationship myself with Baby Kate. She died much too young, before she could even walk. *If only they knew what they had*, I sighed.

"Arrrgh," my daughter grumbled and stuffed the peanut butter and jelly into a paper bag, added an apple, and grabbed her book bag. She didn't even turn her head as she said, "See you later, Mom."

My heart was stabbed. Where did my sweet little girls go? The ones that loved to do whatever I wanted to do. Make cookies, garden, run errands. The ones that kept me so busy doing and thinking for them that I didn't have time to think about myself.

The house was once again peaceful, silent except for Peaches, sprawled on the couch, snoring. She looked so comfy, it made me want to snuggle up to her. Our southern belle we adopted from a bulldog rescue in Georgia after Wilbur died.

I topped off my coffee mug with added fuel and stepped

outside on the back deck. The cold, fresh air forced the fog in my brain to clear. The teak table and chairs were grayed like the color of the shingles on Cape Cod beach cottages. The flower boxes hanging along the railing were filled with wilting impatiens. *My mother would have had them filled with mums or kale and cabbage by now*, I thought. The lawn, which takes over an hour to mow, sparkled with dew. One of the many tradeoffs for moving to Springville, from Nyack, was to get more space. It's hard to believe we live within an hour of the Big Apple.

I walked the stone path to the split-rail fence and eyed the garden. The well-established morning glory vine that Sarah grew from seeds no longer supplied blue and white flowers. The rainbow Swiss chard with its vibrant orange, yellow and magenta pink stalks threw off hardy green leaves. *They should be ready for picking this weekend.* Two pumpkins grew side by side, each one clearly marked with a stake next to it so no one will confuse whose is whose.

A few chickens came clucking around my feet hoping that maybe I would be offering extra feed. "No such luck, you'll have to wait for the girls to get home." They plucked away at the ground searching for worms.

When we first moved to the old farm property, soon after we married, we had big dreams. We would grow most of our own food, including poultry and pork. We started with a half dozen chicks, three goats and a lone pig. The pig turned from a cute, rose-petal pink piglet into a ferocious, filthy, hundred pound plus man-eater. He charged whoever entered the paddocks to feed the animals. Eventually he was too big a risk to have around the girls. It was time for him to go to the butcher.

Jose, our gardener and occasional farmhand, explained that in his native country, the Dominican Republic, they call it a sacrifice when an animal is slaughtered for consumption. A prayer of gratitude is said for the animal. We gave this a try, allowing Jose to lead the prayer before we sent him away. As he drove off in the butcher's truck, Amanda cried, Sarah said good riddance, Luke was more quiet than usual and I apologized to the animal I had come to love, but could no longer excuse. The pork chops, bacon and pigs feet went home with Jose. None of us could bring ourselves to eat an animal we knew. The only things we actually eat from our animals since then are chicken eggs and cheese made from our goats' milk.

As the girls got older they begged for horses. Neither Luke nor I knew a lot about horses, so we sent them to a nearby stable for riding lessons instead. Those were happy years for me. That wave ended just a few years ago. Hanging out with their friends became more alluring than hanging out with horses.

As I rested against the fence I noticed the bright, mustard-yellow spikes of goldenrod rise above the weeds du jour along the back end of the property. They reminded me that I would need to pick up antihistamine for Sarah. She would ceremoniously start sneezing any day.

In the far distance, I heard a siren shrieking, relentlessly. As if I were pushed into a raging river, whose force was too hard to fight, I returned to that tragic night in an instant. I clenched my coffee cup. The only memory I can still remember is driving in the rain on Old Kelley Road, a dark and blustery night. I strained to remember the impact, but couldn't see another car coming. Nothing. The only thing that came was the question. The same question I asked myself every year. *Why didn't I die that night?* Why didn't God take me and leave Samantha's parents to raise her? My mother would have been heartbroken, but she was dying anyway. My dad would have been sad, but he sure seemed to find a way to hold on. Billy, my brother, would have been devastated. But wouldn't it be more important for a baby to have its parents rather than a brother having his sister? I gave in and let the tears flow. The siren faded away. The tears eventually stopped.

Wiping my face dry with my robe sleeve, I took a deep breath and closed my eyes. The crickets played a symphony. The sun shifted above me and I allowed the warmth to prickle my face. A breeze stirred, slowly at first, but then built until the leaves rustled loudly. With the heat of the sun and the roar of the leaves surrounding me, I let my mind wander. It traveled far away, to the tranquil beach on Triton Island. I pretended the rustling leaves were making the sound of waves tumbling onto the sand. I felt a deep sense of calm. *If only I could stay just like this.* I savored the moment until alas the leaves slowly become still. The crickets' song took over again.

Then I heard the sound of a crow.

Chapter 2

AMANDA

Rachel and Kailey stood in front of their open lockers whispering to each other. They separated to allow me to get to my locker wedged in between theirs.

"I overheard Max tell Wendy on the bus this morning that he's going to the Halloween dance," Kailey gushed. Her braces were shiny this morning.

"I wonder what he will go as," Rachel asked, as she organized her books in her locker. She looked in the mirror stuck to the inside door and fluffed her new bangs around. "What are you going to be, Amanda?"

I pulled my notebook out for my first period class: Special Ed Reading. My pencil was going to need sharpening. I shoved the rest of my duffle bag inside the locker, shut the door and spun the lock.

"I'm not sure yet." I answered. Truth was, I wasn't sure if I even wanted to go to the Halloween dance. I would only be subjecting myself to torture watching all the popular girls dance with Justin. He didn't even know I existed, even though we shared the same chemistry lab table.

The first period bell rang and the kids in the hallway scurried like mice.

"We'll see you later, at lunch," my friends said at the same time as they headed off to regular English class together.

I hated the word "special." I didn't feel special at all. I felt weird. Why my brain chose to scramble letters was beyond me. My parents actually looked relieved when the testing showed I was dyslexic.

"They have special classes for that," my mother immediately reacted when she got the news back when I was in third grade.

At first it wasn't so bad. Instead of teachers getting frustrated and my parents telling me to concentrate when I couldn't figure out words, I began to learn to read in my own way. And I was allowed to listen to books instead of read them. When it came time for tests, my teachers scheduled special test sessions where I would be asked the questions and allowed to answer them verbally. But my brain never got normal like my friends. It's embarrassing to have to go to a "special" class.

I tried to talk to my mom about it before school started this year but lately she seemed spaced out and cranky. Dad is always talking about how busy he is at work, so I didn't want to bother him. Forget Sarah—she's so full of herself, especially since she started dating the captain of the lacrosse team. Alex this and Alex that. Gag me.

Chapter 3

JILL

The hallway floors still glistened from the hardcore cleaning and polishing the school janitors did over the summer break. Even the trampling of grammar school feet filled with mud and rain had not yet worn them down. I enjoyed the tranquility while it lasted for it would be filled with the rambunctious chatter of little people, ranging in age from five to seven in just a few minutes.

I jiggled the lock on my office door gently at first. The more it resisted, the harder I turned the key in frustration. I held back from kicking the door for fear of someone seeing the rage building inside of me. Eventually I just backed away, sighed, and cursed the damned lock under my breath. I knew I was overreacting on some level and to be honest, I began to worry where this tempestuousness was coming from lately.

"I can change that lock for you, Nurse Cooper," Wiley said as he inserted himself between the lock and me like a referee. His big hands gently pulled the door towards him and with a gentle nudge the key turned and the door opened.

"Thank you, Wiley. You may have just saved that stupid lock from an all-out assault," I said.

He smiled proudly. Wiley was a graduate of the cooperative education program in our school system. The youngest of the janitors, he worked the hardest, never taking his mandatory breaks.

The older guys kept an eye out for him. I'd hear them jokingly say, "Stop showing us up, Wiley. Come on to the break room with us for a hot chocolate."

"You're right, Wiley. It may be time for me to give in and get a new lock. It wouldn't be good if there were an emergency and I couldn't get into my office."

"I'll take care of it today, Nurse Cooper," and off he went.

Nurse Cooper. When Luke and I married, I dropped my maiden name, Bradley, and took his. I went through identity confusion at first since everyone I knew, knew me as Bradley. Here at the school they have only known me as Jill Cooper.

Luke and I decided that making the career move from mother-baby hospital nursing to becoming a school nurse was best for our family despite the steep pay cut. Having the same hours and schedule as our girls allowed us more quality time together as a family. When Amanda went into middle school, I entered the grammar school of our local school system, giving us all a little space.

Luke's accounting practice was growing. When Package That signed on as a client, our financial portfolio began to blossom. It was comforting to know that someday we may be able to retire. We sure weren't going to be able to on my salary. But, I wouldn't do anything else.

I flicked the light on and laid my bag on my desk. It would have been nice to have a window to the outside in my office rather than being in the center of the building, but I improvised by decorating the window to the hallway with seasonal images. Pumpkins with different faces cut out adorned them now. Amanda helped me make them.

I scrubbed my hands and prepared the morning meds so they would ready to be distributed to the kids who relied on them. Insulin for Ian who just learned he was a juvenile diabetic, inhalers for the kids with asthma and the bunches of pills aimed at trying to help those with autism and ADHD. I thanked God every day that my own children were healthy and that there was something to help treat these kids. They were so brave. Their parents were often the difficult ones to deal with, rightfully so, because the threat of losing their children, or having kids that weren't "normal" was always gnawing at them. Sure, Amanda had dyslexia, but she was well integrated into the mainstream.

The hallway ignited with life as the kids barreled down it like the running of the bulls.

"Good morning, Nurse Cooper." Some students were kind enough to say as they passed by me standing in my doorway.

"Good morning, Leon." I waved my hand. "Tina, wait, let me help you tie your shoe."

Tina stopped and looked down, her oversized backpack weighing her down. I was just reading an article in one of my nursing journals about how these oversized backpacks were causing neck, shoulder and back injuries in school age children. Note to self: incorporate this into one of my upcoming newsletters.

"How is your new baby brother?" I asked Tina while she stood patiently and let me tie her shoe.

"Good," she wiped her nose. "He cries a lot."

Tina was still getting over her cold. I spoke to her mother last week when I needed to send her home with a fever. It took her mom two hours to come and get her. When she did come she was wearing a baseball cap over probably unwashed hair, no makeup.

"I'm so sorry. It took me so long to get here. Tina's father is traveling for work. The baby has colic," she rambled on as she whisked her daughter away. I remember those kind of days all too well.

"I bet you're a good big sister." I tapped her on the head. She shook her head yes, and then ran off to catch up with her buddy, Jenny.

Being present and mingling with the kids was my favorite part of the day. It allowed me easy access into their lives, into their thoughts, much the same way it was when I had to make patients' beds in the hospital. Although a tedious task, that certainly didn't require a degree. It stimulated casual chit-chat which sometimes led to gathering important medical information.

Little Tommy Kindor approached me with eyes full of tears and his bus driver right beside him. "He tripped while going down the stairs to get off the bus."

Tommy held his hand on his right knee. I ushered them into my office and asked Tommy to sit in the chair against the wall.

"Let me see?"

I rolled up his pants to expose his knee. It didn't look bruised or abnormal. I asked him to raise his leg, and then lower it. He didn't wince.

"How about we put some ice on it for a minute and then a Band-Aid? I think you're going to be fine."

He wiped his tears with his sleeve while I retrieved an ice pack. His concerned bus driver stood and waited.

"He'll be fine." I assured him and sent him on his way.

As I placed the ice pack on Tommy's knee, the phone rang.

"Just hold this here for a minute," I said as I reached for the phone.

Tommy nodded okay.

"Hello?"

"Just wanted to let you know that I'm sending Jacob Trough down to see you," Elaine McDowell, one of the second grade teachers told me.

I listened to Jacob's latest escapade.

"He tried to take a box of crayons out of his neighbor's desk without asking and got the desk top slammed on his hand."

Jacob had boundary issues and the kids in his class were always defending themselves from his obtrusiveness.

"Thanks for the heads up," I hung up the phone and grabbed another ice pack from the closet. "Let's see how it feels now." Ever so gently, I removed the ice pack from Tommy's knee.

"I feel better," he said as he took a look.

"What color Band-Aid would you like?"

He looked in my Band-Aid box and surveyed his choices. "Green."

I bandaged him up and sent him off to class. I made a note on a fresh chart with his name and date. I would finish documenting his injury after I dealt with Jacob.

And so the morning went, in and out, the mildly wounded came. The kids were so cute and for the most part easy to repair. Then Shana showed up.

In a quiet whisper she uttered, "I don't feel good." Her soft, smooth face was expressionless, her eyes gazing downward.

"Come in, Shana," I gave her a little hug and let her sit in the chair right next to my desk. I didn't have to ask her what was wrong. I already knew, we all did, and it broke our hearts. It was the invisibly wounded ones like Shana that were so challenging to try and help. The ones like Shana, who resonated with my own life experiences, made it difficult to stay on the side of the street called empathy, rather than sympathy.

Shana's mother and two sisters died a month ago in a house fire. Shana and her father went to get milk, while the rest of the family stayed home to bake brownies on a Sunday afternoon. When the two of them returned, the house was ablaze. Shana's dad jumped out of the car and attempted to run into the house. He sustained second-degree burn injuries before the firemen could get to him. Shana just went into shock. Her father was still in rehab, but expected to recover well. Her grandmother, who lived nearby, took Shana in. We were told it was a gas leak in the kitchen stove that caused it.

"Do you want to draw or listen to music?" I asked Shana.

She shook her head no.

"You are welcome to sit here with me as long as you like."

The school psychiatrist, her teachers and the Trauma Coordinator from the hospital all agreed the best thing for now was not to pressure Shana into talking about the tragedy, but let her process the trauma at her own pace. These kids, who knew the pain of grief way too early in life, broke my heart.

We sat together in silence except for the sound of the second hand skipping around the clock. Minutes went by. In the awkward silence I finished my charting, looking over at Shana every few minutes as she just stared at the cinderblock-painted wall behind me. *God, Shana's mother, someone, please tell me what to say to this poor child*, I prayed in silence.

I thought back to when my own mother had first passed away. What helped, what didn't? Although everyone was well meaning, people who insisted on sharing their own mother's dying experience with me didn't help. It felt like they were piling their own grief onto mine. I remembered feeling at the time like one of those poor sharks whose fins are stripped for soup, and then thrown back in the ocean left unable to swim. I relished in the stories from people who knew my mother. It felt like it kept a part of her alive. I even learned things about her that I never knew.

I couldn't just let her sit there in a trance. I braced myself, daring to tread into her sacred space, and asked

17

Shana, "What did you like to do with your mother that was special?"

She sat still, unaffected. I looked at her patiently, without expectation, but with curiosity and compassion. When the engagement felt burdensome, I returned to my charting.

"Make cookies," I heard.

My head flew up, much quicker than I wanted it to.

Shana was still staring at the wall.

"Yummm, what kind of cookies?"

"Sugar cookies."

My mind began to fire off ideas. We could make cookies. Gosh, I hope her mother didn't have a special recipe.

"Did you make the batter in a mixer?"

Shana looked at me, directly, eye to eye, like I was crazy. "No, we got the cookie batter in a tube at the grocery store. Why would we make all that mess when it was the same thing?"

I chuckled, this was surely Shana's mother talking and I instantly liked her. I never had the opportunity to meet her. "You are absolutely right, those are the best kind."

The final bell ended our conversation. I felt frustrated, like I just discovered a secret treasure, but couldn't open it. I would have to wait until after the weekend.

Chapter 4

AMANDA

Me Text: *I told you why, I think Lady Gaga is stupid.*

Rachel Text*: Come on, don't be such a loser, it will be swag!*

"Girls, you didn't set the table yet. Your mother will be home any minute with the pizza," Dad shouted from the kitchen.

"You didn't make the salad yet," I countered, as I lay on the couch. Sarah didn't bother answering from the La-Z-Boy chair where she was texting, probably to Alex.

Rachel Text: *Are you still there?*

Me Text: *Yeah, I gotta go, though. I'll see you guys tomorrow at the River.*

Rachel: *OK, see you tomorrow.*

"Come on, Sarah, you have to help too," I said as I stood up and slid my phone into my back pocket. Dad was scurrying to gather salad plates with a head of iceberg lettuce in one hand. He laid the four plates along the counter, pulled the outer layer of lettuce off and dropped it into the trash.

"You're supposed to put that in the compost bucket," I scolded him.

"Don't say anything," he went over, plopped the lettuce on the cutting board, took a cleaver, and chopped it into fours. Then he dashed to the fridge again, buried his upper body inside and came out with four pieces of raw bacon lying over his hand. He lay them down on a paper towel and tossed into the microwave. Beep, Beep.

"You're supposed to wash the lettuce," I told him as I pulled out four dinner plates and four sets of knives and forks.

Dad shot me a look then yelled for Sarah, "Sarah, get off the phone and come in here, please."

He wiped his hands on the dishcloth then went back into the fridge, grabbed a bottle of blue cheese dressing, and drizzled some on each of the lettuce chunks. Ding! He bolted back to the microwave as I laid the plates on the table, folded a napkin to put beside each plate and placed the knife and fork on either side.

"Oww." He tossed the hot greasy paper towel on the counter and began to hack at the bacon slices. He then sprinkled them on top of each of his salad creations. "Sarah!"

The back door flung open and Mom blew in like a gust of wind with a large pizza box in her hand. "Wow, look, you have everything ready."

Sarah strolled into the kitchen, took a look at the table then went to get four glasses. "Water?"

"Sure, water will be fine," Mom answered as she headed to the coat closet leaving the cheesy, fresh baked pizza aroma to taunt us.

Dad proudly placed his salad plates next to each of our

settings at the dinner table while he shot me a warning look that said, "Don't say a word."

"Sarah, is the game tomorrow home or away?" Dad diverted the conversation.

"I got half plain, half pepperoni, what would you like?" Mom asked cheerfully, as she went to open the pizza box.

"Home," Sarah sighed.

At that word, Mom stopped and the smile drained from her face. She stood there holding the top of the box half opened in a trance.

"We're playing the Cougars—they're number two in the division."

I listened to Sarah, as did Dad, but kept my eyes on Mom who still just stood there with a blank look on her face, frozen. "Mom, are you okay?"

Now Sarah and Dad were looking at her too. Then we all looked at each other. Then back at her.

"Mom." This time I said it louder and it seemed to shake her up.

She turned, looked at us blankly, and then returned to the task of serving the pizza.

"Mom, are you okay?" Sarah asked again.

"I'm fine," she said curtly. "Dammit! I swear that Adler boy is stoned. He didn't cut the pizza into slices again." She huffed over to the utensils drawer and fished around until she found the pizza cutter. She rolled the cutter across the pie with force and held up a slice, "Who wants plain?"

Dad grabbed his plate and hurried over. Then Mom went to roll a second slice like she was wrestling an alligator until she screamed, "Dammit!" again, and now held up her hand with a finger oozing blood.

"Mom! You're getting blood all over the pizza," Sarah cried.

Dad grabbed the towel he had just used a few minutes ago to wipe his greasy hands on and brought it over to Mom. "Are you okay?"

"Yes, yes, I'm fine." She accepted the towel and wrapped her hand like a mummy. "I'll be right back; I just need to get a bandage."

Mom ran out of the kitchen and we heard her pound her way up the stairs. Dad and I looked at each other concerned, while Sarah went over to survey the pizza for contamination.

"Good, she didn't get blood on it," she finished off the slice Mom was cutting and put it on her plate.

Dad left to go check on Mom and I went over to get a slice before all the plain ones were gone. Slowly, I rolled the pizza blade through the dough like a cutting boat does through the ice on the Hudson River when it freezes. The cheese clung to the sides and gathered in a mass at the point. I tore it off and dripped it into my open mouth as if I were a baby bird accepting a meal from its mother. I went ahead and sliced the rest of the pie hoping to avoid further injury.

I joined Sarah at the table, each of us sitting across from one another in silence. Sarah had already started eating. I thought I should sit and wait. Maybe put the rest of the pizza in the oven to keep in warm. "I sure hope she's okay."

Sarah swallowed, put her slice on her plate and picked

up her ice water. "I'm sure she is. She's a nurse."

"But did you see her just standing there, staring?" I whispered to my sister. "She is acting a little weird lately."

Chapter 5

JILL

Blood began to ooze through the towel that I had wrapped as tightly as I could around my hand. Luke was barreling up the stairs. I had precious seconds to unwrap the towel and assess my injury before he showed up. The last thing I needed was for him to pass out.

I put my left hand in the bathroom sink and gently let water wash away the blood. It was a clean slice, not too deep, but deep enough to require at least some butterfly stitches. Before I could wrap it up in a clean towel, Luke was at the doorway panting.

"Are you okay?" he asked as his eyes widened. He began to wobble.

"Sit down, quick, before you pass out," I commanded.

Wearily, he sank onto the open toilet seat.

Plunk!

"Shit," he said as he folded forward to let his head rest on his knees.

I wrapped my hand with the hand towel draped on the rack. "Was that your phone?"

"Yup," he mumbled.

"Ugh," I added. "You better get it out quick before it fills with water and dies."

He lifted his head just a tad and looked at me. "Can't you do it?"

"No!" Really? Did I need to tell him I was trying to fix my wound?

"But you're a nurse," he added like he was a child, not my husband.

"So that means I like going fishing for cell phones in toilets?" I applied more pressure to the cut area and held my hand above my heart.

Slowly, without admitting defeat, he stood and then looked into the toilet. There, right at the bottom, sure enough was his phone. I waited and watched. He looked at it, but did nothing. Then he announced, "I'll be right back."

"Where are you going?"

He didn't answer. He just ran back downstairs.

I fumbled around in the medicine cabinet. Neosporin, butterfly stitches, gauze, medical tape. I prepared my supplies for my procedure laying each needed piece on the towel on the bathroom counter. Again I unwrapped my hand, rinsed it with soap and let water flush it out good, then patted it dry. One by one I applied the butterfly stitches, and then oozed a thick strip of Neosporin right over the wound edge. With firm pressure, I wrapped the area with gauze then sealed it with tape.

When I looked up in the mirror I didn't recognize the person staring back. She looked lost, scared, tired. This nightmare had to end. Before I could figure out how I was going to get myself back, Luke was tromping back up the stairs. This time he carried a stainless steel shaft with a rubber handle on one end and a cup-like device at the other.

"What is that?" I asked.

He pulled the telescopic handle and it extended several feet. "A golf ball retriever," he answered as he eyed the object he intended to retrieve from the toilet. "I use this when I hit the ball into a pond."

I shook my head.

He began to fish. As he did so, the other end nearly hit me in the head.

"Hey, watch it." I ducked.

He waved the wand in every direction, mumbling, "Shit. Shit. Shit," with every failed attempt.

It was clear from my vantage point this wasn't going to work. I waited for him to give up. He gave it a good try, I must admit. Then he withdrew the device and laid it against the wall.

Frustrated, I leaned in with my unaffected hand, grabbed the phone and handed it to him. "Here, this is ridiculous."

With just two fingers he took the phone and rinsed it off in the sink. No matter what buttons he pushed, it was lifeless. He looked at me defeated.

"I hear baking it on low in the oven in a bag of rice works." I shrugged.

As he looked at my hand, he began to chuckle. "Some nurse I would make."

I smiled, agreeing.

"Are you okay?"

"Yeah, I'll be fine."

* * *

We caught the girls whispering to each other when we returned to the kitchen. They clammed up quickly.

"Just sit down, I'll get the pizza," Luke said. The girls had reheated most of the pizza. So considerate.

"Are you okay?" the girls chimed.

"Fine," I sat down and started up conversation as if nothing had happened. "Have you girls decided on your costumes for the Halloween dances?"

Sarah lifted up her limp slice of pizza, and bit into the tip. Luke delivered a pepperoni slice to my plate, then to the girls and then finally dove into his.

"Alex and I are going as a mermaid and a pirate," Sarah announced.

Luke choked, started coughing and placed his napkin over his mouth until he could breathe well enough to take a sip of his water. He usually reacted something like this whenever Sarah mentioned Alex.

"He's gonna be like a Johnny Depp pirate. Mom, can you help me make a tail? I want to sew lots of sequins to my blue leotard and I'm thinking of dying my hair seafoam green and adding glitter to it." she leaned forward, each of her hands resting on the table beside her plate.

"Sure, maybe we can work on it Sunday," I replied and cut a tomato in half with my fork. Luckily, the cut finger was on my left hand not my right. "How about you, Amanda, what are you thinking of being?"

She took a big bite of pizza as if to buy time. Everyone chewed and waited. She started lifting her pizza aiming for a second bite. I stared harder. She stopped.

"I don't know," she mumbled. "Rachel and Kailey have this dumb idea to go in different Lady Gaga costumes. You know, we would each dress as one of her different personas."

"That's kind of a cool idea," Sarah chimed in.

Of course, she would take the opposing view.

"I don't know, we'll see."

With that, Peaches waddled in and did a downward dog stretch on the kitchen floor while releasing a toxic, colorless fume. We each rushed to grab our napkins using them as gas masks.

"Ewww, Peaches!" we chimed as she sweetly looked at up at us her eyes asking, "Can I have a piece?"

Amanda smirked.

Chapter 6

AMANDA

"I'll be back at twelve o'clock to pick you up, please don't be late," said my mother. I hopped out of our loser cruiser. We weren't babies anymore. Why couldn't she get a regular car now like our friends instead of the minivan?

"Okay, I won't."

She tilted her head.

"I promise." I added and slammed the door.

Rachel and Kailey were waiting on the dock of the boathouse with their paddles in hand. As usual, no Lauren. It was way too nice of a day to sit around and wait to see if she would show up. I waited all week to get out on the Hudson River.

I tromped down the wooded trail layered thick with pine needles. They felt extra spongy and musky smelling, probably from the rain last night. I unzipped my fleece. I was excited to get out and kayak. Free from school. The boathouse porch creaked and the bell above the door jingled as I entered.

"Good morning, Mr. Trevor," I said as I headed for a locker to store my things, including my cell phone. We all learned a hard lesson when Rachel's phone flooded with water after a splash attack we had over the summer.

"It's a great day to kayak, Amanda," he said in his cheery tone. He poured a new pot of water into the coffee maker. There were a lot of old timers who got up early to head out onto their boats to fish even though Mom said she would never eat fish from the river because of the PCBs in it. "I have a kayak and paddle out back for you already."

"Thank you," I replied and ran out back. My parents got me a kayaking membership to the boathouse as a Christmas present last year knowing how much I loved the water. When my friends heard, they convinced their parents to get them one too. My parents were happy about that because we could go out as a group and they wouldn't have to come with me.

"I'm not waiting for Lauren," I announced as I lugged my kayak to the dock. We only had the kayaks for two hours. I didn't want to waste any of the time.

"But what if she shows up?" the other two replied.

"Well, she'll have to paddle out and find us. Last week we waited for almost an hour and she never came."

"But we're not supposed to go out there alone," Kailey whined. She looked up to the top of the hill, hopeful that Lauren would be up in the parking lot.

"I'm going out," I slid my kayak into the water and got myself seated. I snapped my life preserver on and began to paddle. A gentle breeze whispered by my ears. The plunk of the paddle hitting the water made me relax. After several strokes I turned and looked back at the dock. Those two were still there, waiting, talking with their arms crossed.

"I'm just going to paddle around, I won't go far. I'll stay along the shore," I shouted to them.

They turned and Rachel shouted, "Okay!" back to me.

The sun got brighter and I had to strain my eyes. I sat still for a moment, looking at the colorful foliage that climbed the hills on both sides of the river. Then I turned the kayak and paddled upstream with the Tappan Zee Bridge behind me. A few powerboats buzzed around way in front of me. I paddled closer to the water's edge just to be safe. I looked over the side hoping to see a fish or maybe even a turtle. Instead I saw old logs and rocks lining the bottom of the murky water. I laid my paddle across my legs and let my kayak bob in the water like a rubber duck in a bathtub.

"Phooosh."

Silence.

"Phooosh."

Silence.

I willed my ears to detect where the sound was coming from.

"Phooosh."

Then I saw it, a slick shiny gray thing floating up against the rocks just twenty feet ahead. I paddled quickly to it. My heart began to pound.

There was no mistaking what it was. A dolphin. I pulled my kayak up to it, just a few feet away. It lay there floating, half on its side, its eye focused on mine when it saw me. I looked around quick, but there was no one. I wanted to scream for help, but my mouth wouldn't open. My eyes became fixed on the dolphin's eye. I stared into the dark black ring that sat close to the edge of its mouth. It seemed like it was smiling. We stared at each other. I wondered what it was thinking. I felt like it had so much to say.

"Oh," I said out loud. "Are you okay?"

It didn't make any acknowledgement; it just continued to lie there hitting into the rocks with every wave from the wake of boats passing by far in the distance. I paddled my kayak carefully next to the shore, trying not to scare it. I hoisted myself out, and scaled the slimy rocks covered in algae, leaving the kayak to fend for itself. The dolphin's eye followed me. A sliver of the white part showed. I wanted to run, but my feet were bolted to the ground. Gradually, I tip toed closer to it.

"Phooosh."

Kneeling down next to it, my heart saddened. "Are you hurt?"

"Phooosh," softer yet.

Slowly I reached my hand out until it lay on its skin that felt like a just peeled hard-boiled egg. "It's okay, I'll help you."

"Phooosh."

A crow started squawking really loud behind me. It wouldn't shut up. The shock of finding a dolphin there, in the Hudson River, miles from the ocean, wore off, my adrenaline kicked in. Realizing I didn't have a clue what to do, I gently backed away, although I felt like the dolphin wanted me to stay. It gave me that look, the sad one. The same one Peaches gives me when I go to school. I had no choice. I ran down the path along the river towards the boathouse as fast as I could. The pathway gravel crunched beneath my feet.

"Help, help! I need help!"

The girls met me halfway along the path with Mr. Trevor doing his best to follow.

"What's wrong?" they chimed together.

Gasping for breath, I squeaked out, "A dolphin … there's a dolphin up there." I pointed. "I think it's sick."

Rachel turned to Mr. Trevor and repeated my statement more clearly. "Amanda says there is a sick dolphin up there."

Mr. Trevor stopped and put his hands on his waist. "Okay." He took a deep breath. "I'll go call Marine Patrol, and meet you over there. How far up?"

"Not far." My breath got more normal. "Just past where the rock formations start."

My friends and I turned and ran in the dolphin's direction while Mr. Trevor headed back to the boathouse.

* * *

"It really is a dolphin!" Rachel stopped in her tracks with her mouth wide open.

"Oh, the poor thing, why is it just lying there floating on the water?" Kailey put her finger in her mouth and started gnawing on a fingernail.

"I don't know," I said as I crawled back down and sat next to it.

"Don't touch it!" Kailey barked, but it was too late, I was already gently petting its side.

"Phooosh. Click, click, click."

"Should we turn it over and nudge it out to see if it can swim?" Rachel asked as she inched her way closer.

"No, I think we should just wait for the Marine Patrol to get here. I'm sure they will know what to do."

And there we sat for what seemed like forever. We didn't talk, but I felt like the dolphin was communicating with me. It seemed to calm down. Its eye closed just a little, although it never stopped looking at mine. Its breathing slowed down. Rachel took off her favorite purple fleece and wedged it between the dolphin and the rock it kept hitting. It stayed still the whole time.

Kailey called, "Someone's coming!"

We heard stomping coming from the path. A police officer shouted, "Step back, girls!"

"But it's hurt or sick," Kailey told him.

"I said step back," he commanded as he started roping off the area with bright yellow police tape. "The Marine Patrol will be here any moment and they said to stay away from the dolphin."

I patted the dolphin one last time, knelt down close and whispered, "Please hang in there, help is coming." I could have sworn it leaked a tear from its eye.

Sarah, of course, would later tell me, "That's impossible. It was probably just some water that splashed near its eye from the river."

The policeman made us stand outside the yards and yards of yellow police tape. Really? I wanted to say, but didn't dare for fear that I would piss off the cop further and he would force us to leave. I felt so helpless. Kailey started to cry. The poor dolphin started making more "Phooosh" noises. The cop stood with his arms crossed. It took a long time, but eventually a boat came whizzing towards us with a red light twirling on the top.

Mr. Trevor jogged up to us just as the boat reached the shoreline. He looked over our shoulders at the dolphin. "I haven't seen one of those around here in years."

"Why would it swim up the river?" Rachel turned and asked.

"I don't know."

A rugged guy lunged off the bow of the boat over the rocky edge right up onto the shoreline. A shorter nerdy guy followed behind him. The guy driving the boat threw a rope at them. The rugged guy tied it to a tree. The driver throttled the boat trying to keep it from crashing into the rocks. Rugged guy walked up to the dolphin and looked at it. "Yup, it's in distress." And he reached back pulled a walkie-talkie out of his pocket. "Dolphin in distress, approximately one mile north of the Tappan Zee Bridge in the Hudson River on the west shoreline, do you read?"

"Copy that, stranding team has been dispatched."

The two guys leaned in and whispered to each other. One studied the dolphin while the other came to talk to the cop standing near us, still guarding the yellow tapeline like we were at a One Direction concert. We heard him say, "The stranding team is on its way, but it may take a while for them to get here. I'm not sure if they are coming from the station in Connecticut or Long Island. It's probably best if you clear the area," he added as he turned.

"But we found the dolphin," I cried. "I want to stay!"

"I'm sorry, it's best for the dolphin if you leave, we need

to keep it as calm as possible," he said gently, but firmly.

"But—"

Mr. Trevor placed his hand on my shoulder, "Come on, Amanda, let's go wait at the boathouse."

I dug in my heels and my tears flowed.

The rugged guy reached in his back pocket and pulled out his wallet. He walked to the edge of the tape. He slid a business card out and handed it to me. "Look, this is going to probably take several hours. We are going to do everything we can for the dolphin, but it really is best for it to have as few people directing its energy away as possible. If you want, give me a call tomorrow and I'll give you an update."

I took the card, and looked at the dolphin one last time. "Can I just say goodbye to it?" I managed to choke out.

He looked over to Mr. Trevor with pleading eyes.

"Come on, girls, we really must go," Mr. Trevor rounded us up. We walked away, all three of us crying.

Chapter 7

JILL

Amanda's kayaking in Nyack became my excuse to stop and say hello to my father who still lived there in our hometown. Our relationship was cordial, but still uncomfortable since the harsh betrayal I felt after Mom died. I knocked on the back door, heard a "Come in" and entered the kitchen.

"Hi, Dad."

"What was the name of that island you went to?" my father asked from behind *The Wall Street Journal.*

I helped myself to a cup of coffee, and then searched for half-and-half in his kitchen fridge. If my mom were still alive it would have been stowed on the top shelf, right in front. My father's new wife, however, drank her coffee black so it was hit or miss if there would even be any. Today was a miss so I settled on the skim milk on the bottom shelf.

"You mean Triton?" I replied as I poured the milk into my coffee until it was a light mocha color.

He didn't answer; he kept himself buried in the newspaper that gently rested on his protruding belly, also compliments of his new wife, Lois. Lois, being Italian, loved to cook. She introduced us to pasta we had never heard of before. My mother, Helen, was more of a meat and potatoes kind of cook. We'd have spaghetti and meatballs or lasagna on a rare occasion during the cold winter months.

Lois, however, believed in pasta year-round. My father was clearly her best customer.

"Why do you ask?" I leaned against the counter and took a sip of my lukewarm coffee.

My father released the paper onto the kitchen table and pulled his reading glasses off. "I've been told that there are some good investment opportunities there. I'm thinking about taking a trip there to check it out."

Triton. I never got the chance to return there, although I longed for a tropical vacation. It wasn't the utopia I was looking for when I escaped there years ago. It did, however, catch my fall. The people and the natural beauty of the island helped me reshuffle my head after so much tragedy, loss and betrayal invaded my life.

Triton, where I discovered I could love again. Endorphins flooded into my veins and boosted my mood. I hid behind my coffee cup somewhat ashamed of the thoughts I was having about Bane. *Whatever happened to him*, I wondered. Becky and Dr. Sol were the only two people that I told about him when I returned.

I know people would constitute one week of romance as a fling, which really wasn't my style. I did a lot of things I never would have done normally in my gut-wrenching state of grief. My time with Bane was a genuine connection that due to so many circumstances, mostly distance, never could blossom into love, or did it?

"You seemed to like the island from what I remember," my father interrupted my dream state, his eyes now focusing on me. "What happened to your hand?"

I walked over to the table, pushed the newspaper aside, put my coffee mug down and sat in the chair next to him. The clock hanging on the wall behind him ticked. It was the clock that hung in my mother's kitchen and brought some sense of warmth to my father's new home.

Soon after Dad married Lois, they decided to sell my childhood home and downsize to a condo overlooking the Hudson River. This was just one of the many secondary losses that followed my mother's death. No one to call and chat with, no warm pumpkin bread in the fall, no one to remind me, *You've been like that since you were a baby*; the list went on like dominos in free fall.

Truth is, selling our family home probably helped prevent all of us from wallowing in our grief. I understood that Lois needed a new place to call her own.

Still, it hurts when I do the occasional drive by and see how the new owners ripped out all the azaleas my mother had planted by hand in front of our house and replaced them with non-flowering, sculpted boxwood shrubs.

My father wanted the kitchen clock and the family portrait that was taken on the Cape when we were kids. He hung the portrait in his small office in his new place. I took things mostly from the kitchen; the teakettle, some teacups and Mom's favorite roasting pans. Roasting a beef or turkey in them still makes me feel connected to her. I saved her sewing basket with small squares of a newly started quilt in it. I had great intentions of finishing it, but life got in the way.

My brother, Billy, took the grandfather clock that stood in our foyer and the quilt mom made that always sat folded on the couch in the den. It was the perfect cover to snuggle in on a rainy nap day or movie that went on late into the night. My father donated the rest of the things in our house to St. Peter's church's consignment shop. Most of the ladies who volunteered in the shop knew Mom, so we felt a sense of peace that our belongings would be treated with dignity until they found new homes.

"Yes, I loved it. I have to say; I think Triton is the most beautiful place that I've ever been. Not that I am well-traveled." I raised my left hand and added, "Head on collision with a pizza slicer, I'll be fine."

What kind of investment opportunities could be there? I wondered. As I recalled, a good percentage of the island was designated for preservation by a single wealthy investor.

My father looked at his watch and stood up. "I've got to get to the office."

"When are you thinking of going?" I asked as he put his coffee cup in the sink.

"Next month, probably."

I stood up and took one last sip of coffee before dumping the remainder down the drain. This is the way many of my conversations with my father went since Mom died, touch and go. If I were here with the kids and Luke, it would have lasted longer, but not by much. If Lois were present, she would add to the conversation. It took me over two years to accept that he would never be able to fill my mother's shoes. He would not sit and listen. Not chat for hours. He wouldn't tell me, "Don't worry, it will be fine," when I was worried about something.

Next month. November. Could I go too? Maybe make a family trip out of it? I slipped my orange cardigan sweater on as my mind flirted with the possibility. Eating conch, teaching the girls how to snorkel, long walks on the beach, starry romantic nights with Luke.

"I'll see you later, Dad," I shouted as I pulled the back door closed and he headed for the bathroom. And then it hit me while I waited for the condo elevator to reach the penthouse floor. What if Bane is still there?

* * *

With time to kill before picking Amanda up, I hiked up the hill into town. I needed to get more gauze. Nyack's Main Street was already revving up for the lunch crowd. Years seemed to fade away and I felt like a teenager again surrounded by the familiarity of my hometown.

The town was as eclectic and quirky as it always had been in my memory. These were old mom and pop shops that had survived the sustainability challenge along with some clinging to life. Plus a few new contemporary startups sprinkled in and only one nationally known coffee store. The old-timers frequented the trusted haunts like the long skinny diner that still had the swiveling stools with red leather cushions that lined a Formica counter. The younger crowd plucked away at their devices in the window of the Starbucks.

Koblin's Pharmacy was decorated with ghouls, cobwebs and hay bales. They renamed it "Goblin's" every year for Halloween. Soon after I entered it, I ran into one of Mom's old friends.

"Jill, how nice to see you," Mrs. Spinelli greeted me. Her silver hair was as nicely styled as it was when it was sun drenched blond. She gives me a hug that genuinely conveyed she was glad to see me. "How are you?"

"Good," I told her, then caught her up on what the kids were up to.

"You know, I still think of your mother all the time. I have one of the dolls she sewed still sitting in on a bed in my guestroom."

Mom's handsewn dolls. I had forgotten all about them. I remembered that I had one packed in a box in the bottom of my closet. They were each uniquely made for the recipient. Yellow yarned hair for blondes, brown for brunettes and black for a few Asian and African American friends I had back then. *I will have to remember to take mine out of storage*, I thought to myself.

"Yes, I still think about her too," I said wistfully.

"Charles is waiting for me in the car," Mrs. Spinelli pointed out the window. "I don't drive myself anymore. He gets antsy so I better get going." She smiled and hugged me again and I didn't want her to let go. "It's so good to see you. Thank you for reminding me about those dolls."

She tapped my arm as she walked to the door.

I watched her gingerly get into the car with her husband

who gestured wildly in the driver's seat. Some people have no patience.

The shop was filled with Halloween trinkets and enough candy that would keep a dentist from retiring.

"Jill, what brings you into town?" Mr. Koblin said from behind the pharmacy counter. His glasses balanced on the tip of his nose as he grinned broadly.

"Just killing some time. Amanda is at her kayak club this morning."

"Well, always good to see you." He went back to filling the small brown vial in his hands.

I strolled down the cosmetic aisle, although I didn't really need anything. Then I picked out a box of gauze. The magazine rack provided a good place to hang out. I saw a recipe for stew too good to pass up in *Cooking Magazine*. I headed for the register to pay for it and the gauze.

The old register had been replaced with a new fancy electronic one.

"You've upgraded your system I see," I said to Mr. Koblin while pointing to his new register. The young woman behind the counter said, "Twelve ninety-nine," and placed my purchases in a brown bag.

"Gotta keep up with the times, ya know."

You get 'em, I thought to myself. "I'll see you again soon; we have another week before kayaking season ends."

"Say hello to your dad for me."

I meandered down the street. Frozen yogurt shops had replaced ice cream shops; the flower shop was now selling local honey too, the hair salon where we always got our haircut was now a yoga studio. Fashion boutiques sported the latest trends, the smell of incense seeped out of the new age store. I considered going in there. Maybe they'd have something to make the haunting memories go away, but then decided against it.

The best parts of Nyack are the restaurants. You can literally travel the world via your palate. Japanese, Mexican, Irish pubs, Italian, Thai, and vegan all tempting your taste buds. The different aromas teased my olfactory glands and my stomach began to rumble. It is the Italian restaurant with its fresh garlic simmering in authentic olive oil that trumps all the others. I was a drooling dog now. Across the street was the travel agency. I was curious how much it would cost to go to Triton. I quickened my pace towards it instead of ordering two slices of pizza.

The jingling bell greeted me when I opened the door. I flashbacked to 1995. I was a desperate girl entering this storefront trying to be rescued. *I have made progress.* Look at me now. I'm in control. I'm not trying to escape. But a current still ran through me threatening to pull me under.

"May I help you?" I searched the desks for Marge, the older woman who helped me years ago. I didn't see her or her nameplate on any of the desks.

"Umm, yes," I walked over and sat at the chair in front of a lady with "Barbara" on her desk. "I would like to get some information on travel to the island of Triton over Thanksgiving break. There will probably be at least six of us."

"Triton, lovely island, but not very developed. I haven't sent anyone there in a while," she began to search her computer database.

"That's why I like it."

For the next several minutes we bantered back and forth, flight times, hotel choices, and yes, Sea and Sand Resort is still there. I thanked her and left with a folder of options. I had what I needed to present the possibility to Luke. I hoped he would be game.

* * *

As I pulled up to the parking lot, I immediately knew something was wrong. Two police cars were there, their lights flashing. An officer stood leaning on his front hood. My heart raced as fast as a horse breaking the gate at the Kentucky Derby. "What's wrong?" I shouted as I flung open the door of the car that was still running.

"Ma'am, you can't go down there right now."

"What do you mean? My daughter is down there!"

The cop walked toward me and softened his position. "The girls are okay, they are in the boathouse. They found a wild dolphin along the shoreline." He reached over and took a gentle hold of both of my arms and hyper-exaggerated how I should do some deep breathing. I followed his lead. "I understand; I have daughters myself."

Tears of joy leaked down my face and then I found myself giggling from the surge of adrenaline. "Thank you." I nodded that I was okay. "Can I go see my daughter?"

"Sure, but then you have to come right back up here. No one is allowed down the path." He released my arms and gently backed away.

I nodded again, took a deep breath and stood up

straight. Then I hiked down the rugged trail.

When I entered the boathouse I found the four of them huddled around a table, heads down, silent.

"Mom!" Amanda catapulted out of her chair, ran to me and wrapped her arms tightly around my waist as she pressed the side of her face to my chest. I could feel her sobbing. I just let her release her sadness and stifled my urge to cry with her pain.

Mr. Trevor, his eyes full of concern, walked over and explained the situation. He handed me the card that the Marine Patrol guy gave him. Chuck Moors it said.

"Thank you, Mr. Trevor, we'll let you know more when we hear from him." I checked to see that the other girls had rides coming, which they did. Then I gently led Amanda back up the hill.

Chapter 8

AMANDA

My phone rang but I didn't answer it. I was tired of telling Rachel, then Kailey, the same thing. "No, I haven't heard anything. I left a hundred messages for that guy but he hasn't called me back."

Clouds covered and uncovered the moon all night outside my window. Do dolphins look up at the moon? Do they sleep at night? *Please, God, let her be okay.*

Chapter 9

JILL

"I'm the girl who found the dolphin in the Hudson River yesterday. I am calling to find out how she's doing. Can you please call me? My number is 555-5724. Thank you."

I looked at the clock on my bedside table, 6:10 a.m. Well, at least she waited until 6. Luke was lying on his belly, his face scrunched deep into the pillow, dead to the world.

So much for sleeping in, I said to myself. Gingerly, I rose out of bed and tiptoed to the closet to put my fleece-lined slippers and robe on. The mornings kept getting colder and they were forecasting a cold front that might take the temperatures near freezing later this week. It was probably just as well that I got up early. Carpe diem. We still have a lot to harvest before the hard frost hits.

The stairs creaked as I descended them into the foyer. Sun streamed in the front window. I saw Peaches steadfast in her position on the couch with her big head plopped on top of my favorite throw pillow. *Maybe we'll light a fire tonight.*

I know I was stalling going in to the kitchen where Amanda was. I didn't have a good feeling about the dolphin. I wished that guy, Chuck, had returned her call from last night. He promised her an update. At the same time, I needed to stay positive. They found the dolphin alive. That meant there was hope.

I felt pinned into a corner; an all too familiar feeling that I've experienced as a nurse. Colliding forces between accepting what was going on and hoping it will change. Trying to keep patients and their families' wishes and prayers alive, when experience has told you so many times that the outcome wasn't looking good. With patients, however, I could leave them after my shift in the care of the next nurse who would walk down that path with them. *Today, however, it's my daughter who I must walk the path with, wherever it leads to. I don't know this route.*

I moved closer to the kitchen via the dining vestibule. The tiny area was the original kitchen to the farmhouse. We converted it to an informal place to eat our family meals when we added the kitchen to the house with all the modern amenities. The bay window looks out to a giant copper beach that has been estimated to be over a hundred years old. Its magnum trunk is as wide as I am tall. The purple burgundy leaves had turned golden orange and copper. *Soon it will be bare again.* Many a morning I look out at it while sipping my coffee and wonder what stories it could tell. *What advice would it give me now?*

The kitchen was unusually quiet. It was rare for this house to be so still. I found Amanda sitting at the island counter leaning on her elbows staring at her smart phone. Wasn't it just a few months ago this child was jubilant about that phone?

"No, you're too young to have a smart phone," Luke

and I argued with her.

"But everyone has one!" Amanda countered.

"Everyone? Really?" I turned and looked at her.

"Almost everyone."

"You know, when we were kids there was one phone in the house, plugged into a wall. No answering machine. We didn't spend our whole day talking with our friends on it. Everyone in the family used the same phone. If your grandmother called and you answered it, you had to talk to her for a while before giving the phone to your mother. My mother talked to all my friends, she knew who my friends were," Luke reflected as he tied up the trash and hoisted it out to the garage.

Amanda just rolled her eyes, "Did you have to look both ways before crossing the road in case dinosaurs were passing through too?"

In the end, on her thirteenth birthday we gave in and got her the phone. Sarah hadn't been as insistent when she was that age. The technology advanced so much in just a few years, they wanted more, sooner. Luke and I also had to face the reality that our youngest was becoming a teenager, not a little girl anymore. And worse, we were getting older.

Amanda gazed up at me when I sat next to her, then back at her phone. I gently brushed her long dirty blond hair with my hand. "Any news?"

"No," she whispered still willing her phone to ring.

"Today is Sunday, he may not be working. I'm sure the dolphin is in the rescue center by now being treated by veterinarians."

Silence.

"How about if you and I go to early Mass together and say a prayer for the dolphin?" I learned that even in my most powerless moments to help someone, there was always prayer.

Amanda got up. "I don't want to go to church." She walked out of the kitchen, leaving Chuck's card behind.

God, please don't let this dolphin die.

Years ago the girls won a goldfish at a local carnival. It survived for eight months in our kitchen, in a large rose bowl. The girls named it Goldilocks. The first week they were good about caring for it, feeding it, doing water exchanges, cleaning the bowl. Then it became my job. I'm not sure what I did, or what happened to the fish, but Sarah found it bobbing in the bowl one summer morning.

Sarah was sad, but not distraught. "What do we do with it, Dad?"

"Throw it in the toilet and flush it," Luke replied.

Sarah went to pick up the bowl, but Amanda stopped her. "No! Mom, we can't flush Goldilocks down the toilet! Are you sure she's dead?" she searched arduously for a sign of life.

I looked into the bowl with her. "I'm sorry, Amanda, I don't see her gills moving." Somehow the girls decided Goldilocks was a girl. I never did find out how you can tell the difference so we just went with it. I took the bowl and put it back on the counter. "Why don't we bury it and then its soul will go to heaven."

"That sounds like a better idea," Luke said.

So we all got dressed. Amanda found a shoebox in her closet and decorated it. We lined the box with cotton, placed Goldilocks comfortably in it and did a processional out to the backyard. Luke dug a hole about a foot deep and Amanda laid the box in it. The girls refilled the hole with the dirt and patted it down firmly.

Luke said a prayer—amazing what the man would do for his daughters. "Lord, thank you for allowing us to have Goldilocks be a part of our family. We pray that she rests in peace."

The rest of us chimed, "Amen," and then headed back to the house. All of us except for Amanda, who sat cross-legged right next to the grave.

"Are you coming, Amanda?" I asked.

"No, not yet, I want to watch its soul go up to heaven." She sat there for over an hour, despite my attempt to explain soul and spirit. Eventually, hunger drove her to abandon her mission.

The next morning I awoke to find Luke out in the backyard with a shovel and garbage bag. The shoebox was torn to shreds and puffs of cotton were spread around the yard.

"What are you doing?" I whispered to him as the morning dew seeped into my slippers.

"Damn raccoon must have dug up the fish!" he growled as he picked up the pieces.

I couldn't help but laugh. "I guess that's why they dig six feet down."

"All this is going in the trash," he muttered.

I twirled Chuck's business card in my hand then unplugged my cell phone lying on the kitchen counter and dialed his number. "Hello, Mr. Moors. My name is Jill

Cooper, I am Amanda's mother. I'm very sorry to disturb you on a weekend, but my daughter is very concerned about the dolphin that was in the Hudson River yesterday. If there is any way that you could call us with even an update on its condition, I would greatly appreciate it." I left my number and hung up the phone.

As I went through the coffee making meditation in peace, the phone surprisingly rang with a number I didn't know.

"Hello?" I abandoned the coffee pot.

"Mrs. Cooper?"

"Yes, this is she."

"This is Chuck Moors, from Marine Patrol."

"Yes, Mr. Moors, thank you so much for calling!" I said with a mix of hope and relief.

"I'm glad that you called, because to be honest, I didn't want to call your daughter back, she's so young."

He paused.

I braced myself.

"Mrs. Cooper, I'm very sorry to tell you, the dolphin died. The autopsy showed that it had plastic bags inside its stomach and intestines. They think it died from malnutrition because of the bags. It's a growing problem that we see with marine life these days. There is so much plastic in our seas, lakes and rivers. The animals think it's food and ingest it. I'm really sorry."

My throat tightened. "Thank you, Mr. Moors. I really appreciate you taking the time to call me."

"If your daughter has any other questions, and you think it would help to talk to me or the rescue center, please let me know."

"I will. Thank you, again."

Slowly I placed the phone on the island and held it.

"It died, didn't it?"

I turned to find Amanda in the doorway, her eyes glistening.

"Yes, I'm so sorry, baby." She rushed into my arms again and released the anguish that had built up in her since yesterday. I held her as tight as I could without suffocating her and leaned my cheek on the top of her head, my own tears dripping into her hair.

When the sobbing slowed, I explained to her about the plastic bags. Between the last sniffles she squeaked out, "Can we go to church now and light a candle like we do for Grandma?"

"Sure, honey, go get dressed." I glanced at the clock on the stove, 7:40. "We'll have to hurry to make the eight o'clock Mass."

We scurried as quietly as we could and hurried out the door decaffeinated. A few scattered cars were parked in the church parking lot. Typically only the older folk made it to early Mass. As we entered the sanctuary the rows of blood red colored votives stood with only three candles lit. A statue of Jesus on the cross stood behind it, a kneeling bench in front.

"You go ahead and light your candle and say a prayer for the dolphin." I handed her a dollar to put in the donation box. "I'll wait for you inside." We sat through the service, Amanda more stoic than I thought she would be.

As we left the chapel all of the candles were glowing.

Chapter 10

AMANDA

My stomach was growling so much that I had to admit that I needed to eat even though I didn't want to. Just as I was about to go into the kitchen and pick at lunch, I heard my parents talking. I stopped short and tried to hear what they were saying.

"It will be good for her," I heard my mom say. She was clearly trying to convince my dad about something that had either to do with Sarah or me. I snuck up to the doorway and hid along the wall with my ear as close to the kitchen as I could get without being seen.

"I thought we were going to try and take a family vacation during their winter or spring break next year." My father sounded frustrated. "I know you really want to go to on a tropical vacation. If we go over Thanksgiving break, we can only go for five days. If we wait, we can go at least a week."

"I know, but your mom is planning to have Thanksgiving with your brother this year. Billy is going to Mindy's parents. It will just be us and my dad and Lois. Maybe going away will make it more palatable and fun. Maybe it's time we try establishing some new traditions." I could not see them, but I could picture my mother standing there by the sink, tall and still with her eyes fixed on my father. He was probably scowling because he was interrupted trying to catch the scores on the sports page. He loved reading the Sunday paper.

"What about Peaches?"

I could hear Peaches' collar clanking against her bowl while she chomped down her dog food. The clanking paused for a brief moment, probably as she looked up to see why her name was being mentioned, but she quickly returned to her feast when the distraction didn't include food. Dad was going for Mom's jugular now. We always told her she loves Peaches more than us to try to make her feel guilty and get what we want. It usually just backfires because she says, "Yes, you're right."

Silence. Hmmm, Mom must be thinking. Then, "I could see if Billy would take care of her." Peaches loves our Uncle Billy and vice versa.

Sarah came down the stairs, dressed in her tight jeans and Ugg boots and a new hunter green sweater that made her hazel eyes stand out. I quickly pulled my finger up to my mouth and she got the signal. She tiptoed over to the other side of the door, careful not to creak the old wood floor.

"I just don't think it's a good idea to go Thanksgiving weekend." Dad replied weakly.

"Go where?" Sarah jumped into the conversation. She ruined it! I followed behind her. Mom turned towards us.

"To Triton Island, it's a small island in the Caribbean," Mom told us as she held a glass of water firmly.

"Not on Thanksgiving weekend!'" Sarah howled. "That's the big game between us and the Panthers. I can't miss that!"

Dad stood up now, laid his paper on the table and put his plate in the sink. Clearly a stalling tactic while he thought how to answer. Maybe he had a chance. Dad loved to go to the high school football games; Sarah's cheerleading gave him the perfect excuse. He always claimed he was being supportive of her, but at the end of the game, he talked about the plays, not so much about the new cheers Sarah and her teammates practiced all week.

"Why did you say 'it would be good for her'?" I wedged my way into the conversation while Sarah stood with her arms crossed.

They didn't seem to consider, or care, that we had been eavesdropping. Perhaps being ambushed caught them off guard.

"I said it would be good for you, because there are wild dolphins down there. I thought seeing them would make you feel better," my mother said to me softly.

"They have dolphins there?" I said excitedly.

"Great! More about the dolphins," Sarah stomped her foot and left the room. My parents didn't call out to her or follow her and that worried me. Sarah didn't usually get this temperamental, so they must really be worried about me. Was I moping around that much?

"Yes," my mom said. "They even had one that likes to come up and swim with people sometimes. I don't know if he is still there, but it is a magical place."

My dad looked at me.

Swim with one? That would be just awesome! I held my hands in the pretty please position.

"Okay," Dad said, "we can go."

Chapter 11

JILL

"How was your weekend?" Evelyn asked, as we both walked down the school corridor.

"Busy," I replied. I was half on a high thinking about our trip to Triton coming up next month. The other half of me was burdened with worry, and not just about Amanda. For the third time this week, I awoke having the same nightmare. The real kind, that made you feel like you were really there. "How about you?"

"Good, we took the kids to the haunted corn maze. Gary went in with them. I stayed at the refreshment booth sipping hot cider. Too scary for me," Evelyn shuddered.

"I hear you, I avoid those kinds of things too," I kept walking as she stopped to unlock her classroom.

"See you at lunch," she said.

"Hopefully," I answered when I reached my office door. I gave up trying to predict what kind of day it was going to be. The smell of alcohol pads blasted me when I opened the door.

I sat at my desk for a minute and gazed at the calendar. I flipped it to November and wrote the word TRITON across the dates November 21 through 25, something to look forward to. That is what I needed. That is what we all could use right now. *Call the travel agent and confirm the trip*, I scribbled on my To Do pad. I had enough time to find a substitute so we could leave on Wednesday morning. It will be fun, I told myself. But the chilling effects of last night's nightmare still resonated inside of me.

The morning bell chimed and the stampede began. I snapped into school nurse mode and got busy. No one stopped in with a complaint. They just rushed on by. Good, maybe it will be a calm morning, I told myself. But, I spoke too soon. Just as the last classroom door closed down the hall, Shana appeared in the door.

She held up the doorframe. Her hair was neatly weaved into five cornrows with pink ribbons tied to the end. The ribbons matched her dress, which flared a bit at her knees, not a wrinkle on it. Black patent leather shoes adorned her feet matched with white bobby socks. Her eyes studied the floor.

"Shana, you look beautiful today! Is that a new dress?" I asked and walked closer to her.

She didn't look up. Eventually she murmured, "Yeah."

I kneeled down to her level. "How was your weekend?"

Painful silence. "Good."

Stumped, I stayed in my squatted position while my knees began to ache and waited for her to initiate some conversation. It felt like hours. I gently rubbed her arm dangling on her left side. The right arm lifted to allow her hand to twist the bow on the midriff of her dress.

"Can I sit here?" eventually she pointed at the chair she

sat in on Friday.

"Yes, sure. Does Mrs. Taylor know you are here?"

Her head bobbed up and down, yes.

As she got comfy in the chair, I prepared the morning meds. Every once in a while I noticed her peeking her eyes at me to see what I was doing.

"So, Shana, tell me what kind of cookies you used to make with your mom," I asked in a cheery tone, trying to lighten the heaviness.

"Chocolate chip." She began to wring her hands together, but she looked up at me. "Sometimes sugar cookies."

"Yumm." An idea popped in to my head. I reached out and grabbed Shana's hand. "Come with me?"

A flicker of light came into her eyes. She didn't ask where we were going. She followed right alongside of me. We entered the empty cafeteria and I looked into the window of the swinging door that led to the kitchen. The cafeteria ladies were in there, white hats covering their hair, busy preparing lunch for the ravenous crowd that would soon invade them. I knocked on the window. The one closest to me, Grace, stuck her head through the door.

I didn't have to introduce Shana to Grace, or anyone at the school for that matter. Everyone knew her sad story. But I did anyway.

"Grace," I continued. "Shana and her mother used to bake cookies together. Do you think it would be possible for her to bake some with you tomorrow? She is very good at making chocolate chips." I knew all too well that fresh baked chocolate chips were on the lunch menu every

Tuesday and Thursday. It's quite possible that I was more excited about this than the kids.

Grace looked at me with a warm smile. "I would need to check with our supervisor, but I don't see why not. Would you like that, Shana?"

Shana looked at me first, then Grace and nodded yes. Then she asked, "Can I bring some to my dad?"

* * *

"Aww, poor thing," Evelyn sympathized after I told her about Amanda and the dolphin.

"Yeah, she seems really affected by it. She's such an animal lover," I added.

"I remember being present with my mother when my grandmother died," Evelyn opened a bowl of salad with tuna on top. "I was just a kid, but it was a deep experience. And she was supposed to die."

Supposed to die. I watched as she dug into her salad completely satisfied that her last statement was truth. She caught me staring.

"What?" she said with her mouth full.

For a moment I contemplated whether or not to say anything. Supposed to die? Is anyone supposed to die? Were Samantha's parents, my mother at such a young age, the babies that die every day supposed to die? Wasn't the reality that tomorrow is promised to no one?

Before I could answer, Antonio busted through the door to the teachers' lounge and plopped himself down on one of the couches lining the far wall. He sighed heavily and let his long, firm legs spread out. Evelyn looked at me and rolled her eyes. He was one of the new faculty. A welcome replacement to Mrs. Crouch, the previous physical education teacher, who finally gave in and retired so she could get her knees replaced.

Being bilingual, Antonio was a huge asset to all of us. Although most of the kids spoke English, some of them had parents who only spoke Spanish. Antonio graciously came to interpret whenever we needed him, even during parent teacher night. The kids loved him. He was young and vibrant. Rumors swirled that he almost went pro in soccer in his native Spain. An ankle injury ended his run.

He sighed heavily again, which drew him a few more glances from other the faculty dotting the lounge. I shrugged my shoulders back at Evelyn.

Finally, Mrs. Kolwinski, the principal's assistant asked, "Okay, Antonio, what's bothering you?"

"These kids, they never stop talking!" he held both hands to his head and shook it side to side. This was not the Antonio we had come to know. His Latin vibrancy usually penetrated the room and his humor often had us gasping for air.

"Do you have a headache?" Mrs. Kolwinski asked.

"Headache? *Ai caramba*, I feel like *me cabeza* is going to crack open," he let his hands drop to the side and leaned back until his head rested on the back cushion and he closed his eyes. My ears perked up, but I didn't step in to intervene just yet.

"Maybe you should ask Jill to take a look at you?" Mrs. Kolwinski turned and looked at me curiously.

63

"It will go away," he mumbled. Then he opened his eyes and sat up. "My fiancée, she wanted to go out dancing last night. Dancing, on a school night. We ran in to some friends who insisted on doing some shots of tequila. I didn't get home until 2:30 in the morning."

Evelyn grimaced at me. I raised my eyebrows at her. Been there, done that. I reached into my purse and pulled out a bottle of aspirin. "Here, take two; maybe it will help clear your head faster."

He raised his hands appreciatively like a peasant accepting a loaf of bread. "Do you have a glass of water?"

Gosh, he was bad off. I went over to the vending machine and bought him a bottle of water. He accepted it, popped the pills in his mouth and washed them down. "God bless," then leaned his head back once again and closed his eyes.

When I returned to our table, Evelyn leaned over and whispered, "Poor guy, he won't do that again."

"Nope," I said as I raised my coffee cup to my lips.

Chapter 12

AMANDA

We sat on the wooden bench together behind home plate. Rachel was the only one who could really hit so she was usually in the top five of the lineup. Kailey was much more interested in keeping her outfit clean than getting a home run. I just didn't have good eye hand coordination. So Kailey and I waited until they got to the end of the line up together.

"I'm still really bummed that dolphin died. She was so sweet," Kailey lifted her head and looked at me briefly. Then she looked down again at the dusty dirt below us.

It was a girl. The marine guy told my mom. Most of the school knew about her death and knew it was me who found her. I hated the attention.

The feeling that the dolphin and I had a conversation, without even saying a word, still sat deep inside me. There were no more tears to cry. I think I emptied whatever tank they are normally stored in.

A crow landed on the batting cage fence. It turned its head and looked at me. I felt chills all along my arms as if butterflies were flapping their wings against them. Then it flew away.

"We are going to a place to see wild dolphins during Thanksgiving break," I offered. I wasn't as convinced as my mother that this would magically make my sadness disappear.

"That's cool," Kailey replied.

Rachel ran across home base. I didn't bother to get up and warm up my swing. Tanya stepped up to home plate, swung and missed.

"Strike one!" the other team shouted.

The other side of our bench cheered, "Come on, Tanya!"

Crack! The ball flew over the second baseman and dropped into center field.

As our next player walked up to try to bring Tanya home, Rachel leaned over and said, "You're up next."

I didn't say anything. I didn't get up.

"We're sad about the dolphin," Kailey explained.

Rachel leaned over and let her hands catch her head. "Yeah, me too. That really sucks. Why are people throwing garbage into the ocean?"

"Batter up!"

Everyone on our bench was looking at me. I got up and struck out. Kailey at least hit a foul ball before she struck out too.

Chapter 13

JILL

A wave of anticipatory excitement weaved through my body. In less than four weeks we would be on a plane to Triton. Two nights without nightmares, amazing what a good night of sleep will do. This week was off to a good start after the tragic weekend.

Feeling hopeful, I went to check on how Shana was doing in the kitchen.

"She's a wonderful helper," Grace said.

Shana almost smiled.

"I'm sure she is. Let me know if you want to come back to my office when you're done, okay?"

"Oh no," Grace retorted as she held her hand on Shana's shoulder. "Shana was telling me that her mother wanted her to study very hard so she could be whatever she dreamed of when she got older. So, she is going to go back to class to start learning again." Grace winked at me.

My heart warmed. The resilience of children never stopped amazing me. How could I have doubted her for a second?

Shana looked up at Grace.

"Isn't that right, Shana?"

The young girl looked at me and nodded, assuredly.

"That's wonderful news," I said to them both. "I'll let you get back to your baking." A fresh batch of chocolate chips sat on a large aluminum tray, their chips gooey and inviting. My mouth watered. I turned quickly and headed back to my office to avoid temptation.

Amanda will bounce back too, I told myself. Death is just hard, no matter what age you are. Sudden death, though, is harder to deal with. It's like choosing whether you want to rip a Band-Aid off slowly or quickly. Either way sucks. Your pain can be long and torturous, or a quick, deeper sting. I wish it were true that only old people died.

Chapter 14

AMANDA

The school cafeteria was already half full. Rachel, Kailey, Lauren and I scanned the area for a table with some privacy. A long line flowed out of the kitchen as it usually does on spaghetti day.

"How about over there?" Rachel pointed to the far end of the cafeteria by the windows. The table was empty except for David who sat there alone nibbling on his sandwich while reading. We followed Rachel and claimed the other end of the table. I normally would have just thought what a nerd David was with his thick black glasses and crazy hair. He wore a button down collar shirt but didn't keep a pen in the pocket. He probably didn't need a pen. He probably just typed everything on his iPad instead. Today I noticed something different about him. His lunch was packed in a reusable bag, his sandwich wrapped in foil; he drank from a thermos. He had a fresh piece of fruit for dessert. Maybe he was cooler than I thought.

"I can't wait for Friday." Kailey bit into her tuna sandwich. "What are you guys doing this weekend? Want to go see a movie?"

"Maybe, what's playing?" Rachel replied.

"I'm not sure I can, my sister has a home game." The deal in our family was if Sarah were cheerleading at a home game we would all go and support her as a family. I felt extremely lucky not to have to attend any of her away games.

Lauren leaned toward me and whispered, "Have you talked to Justin yet?"

"No, not yet. I'm trying to think of something smart to ask him in chemistry class." My shoulders drooped. Rachel and Kailey followed my gaze across the room.

"Leave it alone," Kailey warned.

My teeth started to grind together. Half the middle school lacrosse team now sat at the table next to us; most of them with trays full of spaghetti, a slice of Italian bread, small side salad and red Jell-O. Ever since the dolphin died a week ago, I had been bringing a lunchbox with a dolphin on it. Okay, so it was the kind we used in grade school, but I liked it. Harley made it his mission to chide me every chance he could. Harley looked at me and raised his plastic bag, like he was toasting me at a wedding. He pulled his sandwich out tucked in a plastic bag, then his large bottle of soda and plastic-wrapped cookies. I was boiling.

When he winked I lost it.

"Amanda, no, sit down!" Kailey tried to grab my arm but I slipped away to the lacrosse table. Even David lifted his head to see what was going on.

As I ripped the bag away from Harley, he laughed with his friends at me.

I began shaking and screamed, "Don't you know that

these things kill animals!" I grabbed the sandwich out of his hand, threw it to the floor and stomped on it.

"Hey, that was my lunch!" he cried, got out of his seat, walked over to my lunchbox and squished it flat as a tire with his foot. He was lucky he stood a foot taller and weighed at least 60 pounds more than me or I would have punched him. Instead, I reached over to his buddy's plate, grabbed a handful of spaghetti and hurled it at him. That unleashed a food fight to end all food fights. Within seconds, spaghetti and red Jell-O were being flung all over until it splattered the walls and ceiling, dripped from the students' hair, and shoulders while people began hitting the floor like they had slipped on a sheet of ice.

School security guards came in blowing whistles and the lunch ladies shoved students out of any door they could find. Before long it began to simmer down. The cafeteria emptied until it was just Harley and me standing there. I wiped the spaghetti sauce from my eyes. He pulled strands of spaghetti out of his hair as he pointed at me and told the guard standing with his hands on his hips, "She started it."

Mr. Muchio stormed in the cafeteria. "Campbell! Cooper! In my office, NOW!"

As Harley and I marched towards the principal's office, our heads down, I noticed David's lunch bag lying under the table and I felt bad.

Chapter 15

JILL

The call came in just as I was putting my day's charts away.

"Yes, Mr. Muccio, I will come down right now. Is Amanda okay?" I listened and scrunched my face in shame. "I understand, I will be right there."

I grabbed my bag and headed to the parking lot. The last bus was pulling away from the curve. I was glad no one stopped me along the way. Amanda had talked about a boy who had been taunting her about her lunchbox. But she had never acted out in a manner like this. I was even more worried now than I was before.

It's a life changing experience to be with someone who is dying. Even more so, to be one of the last people that a living, breathing soul looks at, eye to eye before they die. My nurse colleagues and I rarely talk about it; it's just "part of the job." But I know from experience that it can be an honor and at the same time a haunting experience, stimulating questions most people don't even routinely think about. How can someone be here one minute and then gone the next? Where do they go? How does it feel to die? On the med-surg unit I used to work on, the staff always looked contemplative and solemn when a patient died. A nurse in the Operating Room shared with me once that she locked eyes with a patient who went under anesthesia for a procedure that he never woke up from. It resonated with her for weeks. There are the stories of the ER nurses who rush to the side of teenagers shot during gang wars who stare at them while they plea, "Am I gonna be all right?" as the life leaks out of their gunshot wounds and their faces turn bluish gray.

My poor Amanda had been exposed to the fragility of life at such a young age and she was alone when she found that dolphin. I can only imagine the exchange between the two although they spoke no words.

As I drove the two miles to the middle school, I pondered what to say to Amanda and the school principal. I considered calling Luke but decided not to. We'll talk about this together later. I knew he said he had a busy day on tap. Then the fury started to rise in me as I thought about what kind of callous kid would taunt Amanda knowing what happened to that dolphin. I don't care what the experts say that sometimes this is how young males show they like a girl. They taunt them to get their attention because they don't know anything else. I saw a cop car hiding down the road and slowed myself down noticing I was going 50 in a 30 zone.

The old brick middle school was mildly buzzing with activity. A group of girls played soccer in the field to the right of it, two teachers stood in front having a conversation. I was lucky to find a parking spot. I double-checked that I had my keys before locking my door. I remembered my posture, kept my head straight and took a deep breath as I headed for the principal's office in my new brown suede one-inch heels.

"Yes, Mrs. Cooper, Mr. Muccio is expecting you." The school office secretary pointed me to an office behind the desk. I noticed another office next to it with a tall boy sitting in a chair. He was covered in spaghetti sauce. He didn't look over, lucky for him. The smell was nauseating—nothing like what came out of the Italian restaurant in Nyack.

I gently knocked on the smoky glass that says Principal's Office in black paint, and then pushed the already slightly ajar door all the way open. I found Mr. Muccio looking up at me from behind his thick wooden desk, cluttered with papers, his hands clenched together as they lay on the felt green blotter. His hair was greasy and thinning. He reached up and pushed his wire rim glasses more firmly into his face, then stroked his beard. He's a heart attack waiting to happen, we school nurses have come to surmise. His approach is tough and he tries to come across as a bull, but the kids all love him. They can see through his façade, and know he only wants the best for each of them.

Amanda sat in one of the two green leather chairs in front of Mr. Muccio's desk. She looked pretty sheepish. I tried to tell her don't worry as I sat in the chair next to hers. I took her hand in mine.

"Thank you for coming so quickly, Mrs. Cooper." Mr. Muccio started out. "Amanda and I have been talking. She has admitted that she threw the first round of food that initiated a food fight. I also understand what provoked her to do so. I am not supporting Mr. Campbell's actions, but I am sure that you understand I cannot tolerate this type of behavior in my school." He looked from me to Amanda.

"Yes, Mr. Muccio, I understand. I hope that you also understand that Amanda has had a very traumatic experience recently and is recovering from that."

Mr. Muccio put his hand up. "Like I said, Amanda and I have been talking. I understand the situation and I empathize with what she is going through. Defacing school property and creating chaos is not going to help the cause of eliminating the use of plastic in our schools."

Amanda's eyes were all red.

"I am going to be talking to Mr. Campbell's mother later today. In the meanwhile, I am going to send the two of them down there with a janitor to clean up the cafeteria. They will miss their afternoon classes and have to stay after school to make up the work. I hope this will not happen again, I don't want to have to take more severe action."

These were the times when working in the same school district as my kids really sucked. I wanted to fight harder for Amanda, argue that Harley should clean the whole thing by himself, but acquiesced. "I'm sure this won't happen again," I affirmed and looked at Amanda who shook her head. Amanda and I stood and left his office.

In the hallway, out of earshot of the office, I hugged Amanda. She pushed me away, "He's killing animals!" she said curtly.

"Amanda, now wait a minute. He's not directly killing animals. He is using plastic. There are millions of people who are. The problem is that like most people he probably doesn't have a clue what the effect on the planet plastic use has, especially when it's not recycled." I gently stroked her hair as she stood with her arms crossed. "I'm sorry he is taunting you. If he continues to do that, you need to alert Mr. Muccio or one of the teachers. Go and get the cafeteria cleaned up and we'll talk about this more when you get home."

She released her arms and kicked at the tile on the bottom part of the wall.

Chapter 16

AMANDA

Mr. Glover handed Harley a push broom and me a bucket with a sponge in it. "Young man, you start in that corner and push all this food into one pile, then we'll pick it up. Damn shame, there are people starving so bad they would eat what's on the floor here; you kids just go throwing it around." He flicked his hand toward the corner of the cafeteria and Harley headed that way, broom in hand. "You, young lady, start in that corner, wipe down all the tables and make sure you get the seats and all the nooks and crannies the sauce has seeped into." He pointed toward the corner opposite of where Harley was. I looked around the cafeteria as I followed my orders like Cinderella. At least the security guards broke up the food fight before it got everywhere, but still it was going to take hours to clean this up.

Mr. Glover looked at the ceiling and shook his head. He pulled a white rag out of his dark green pants pocket and blew his nose in it, wrapped it up, then put it back in his pocket. "I'm going to have to go and get the ladder so you can get that cleaned up." He shuffled out the door and headed down the hall. Guilt crept inside me and mixed with the anger and frustration still brewing toward Harley.

As I wiped the sludge of food off the first table, I sneaked a look at Harley, who was eyeing me while he swept. "You're such a jerk!" I shot at him quiet but fiercely.

He smiled, "At least you're talking to me."

I focused more diligently on my job at hand, forcing myself not to give him any more attention. After ten minutes we found ourselves moving closer. I wished Mr. Glover would hurry up with that ladder. More spaghetti sauce was splattering all over me, the smell was making me sick and I had ruined my new fall orange fleece. "This better come off," I jabbed at Harley as I stood up and pointed at all the stains.

"So, what's up with that first grade dolphin lunchbox anyway?"

"You're too stupid to understand," I bent over to wipe the Jell-O off the seat in front of me and then rinsed the sponge again in the bucket of warm soapy water.

"Try me."

I thought about it for a few minutes in silence. Was it even worth trying to explain to such a stupid jock?

"You know I found a dolphin last week in the Hudson River?" He nodded. "It was barely alive." I wiped the hair back from my face with my forearm. "It ended up dying because it had plastic bags in its stomach. Plastic bags!"

Harley stood in silence, and leaned on the broom handle.

"The Marine Patrolman told me the ocean is full of plastic and it's killing the marine life."

Harley opened his mouth to say something, but Mr. Glover cut him off as he clanked through the door holding a six-foot folded up stepladder. "Young man, why don't you give me a hand with this thing."

They proceeded to set it up and Harley climbed up to pull the spaghetti strands off the ceiling. "I'm going to need to borrow your sponge."

I rinsed the sponge again and handed it to him. "I better go and get some fresh water, this one is filthy."

* * *

It took several hours for us to get the cafeteria cleaned. Mr. Glover stopped periodically to reach and stretch his back. Harley got twenty minutes off to meet with his mom in the principal's office.

"I hope you learned an important lesson today, young lady," Mr. Glover said to me while Harley was gone. "Don't pay no attention to these boys. You just stay focused on your studies. None of them are worth paying attention to."

I nodded my head at him in agreement, but thought about Justin.

"My daddy would have given me a whooping if I did this at school," Mr. Glover announced as Harley came back to continue cleaning.

Harley looked down as he picked the broom up again. "My dad probably won't even know. My parents are divorced, I don't see him much."

With that, we kept to ourselves and finished the job at

hand until the darkness of daylight savings time filled the windows with black. When the last morsel was picked up and every wall, ceiling, floor, table, chair was clean, Mr. Glover let us go.

"Thank you, Mr. Glover, for helping us," we said in unison. We headed out to the cars waiting in front of the school with their lights on. My dad came to pick me up. I knew I didn't have to worry about getting a whooping. I wasn't so sure he wasn't going to whoop Harley as his eyes followed him right until he disappeared in his mom's car. I knew that we would be having a talk, though.

Chapter 17

JILL

"Do you think she needs to see a therapist?" Luke asked as he peeled back the blankets and snuggled into the bed.

"No, I'm hoping not. I really think that Amanda will bounce out of it once she sees Sharky the wild dolphin in Triton," I replied, sitting upright leaning against two pillows with the reading lamp on, skimming through the latest issue of *School Nurse*. *I sure hope that dolphin shows up*, I thought to myself. The idea of not seeing the dolphin was too much to bear, so I didn't even bring it up with her. I needed that dolphin to do to Amanda what it did to me all those years ago.

"Well, she can't keep behaving like this," Luke added, his head resting comfortably now, his eyes gazing up at me.

"Oh, I think she knows that after the talking to we gave her tonight," I closed my magazine and laid it on the table. Luke and I threw every threat we could think of at her if she acted out like that again.

I leaned down and gave Luke a smack on the lips. I pulled away and reached over to turn the reading lamp off.

As I did, I heard, "That's it? That's all I'm gonna get

tonight is a little kiss?"

I turned off the light, snuggled in close to my husband until I could smell the day old scent of him and whispered, "So, what were you thinkin'?"

* * *

"Jill!"

I felt my body being shaken like a chicken in a Shake 'n Bake bag.

"Jill, wake up!"

My eyes popped open. Was I just blasted out of a rocket ship? Luke had a strong grip on my left arm. My heart was trying to get out of my chest. My hair was clammy with sweat. I started to re-enter reality. I took a deep, relieved breath and sat up. Luke reached over and turned his bedside light on. We squinted at each other.

"What's going on?" he looked concerned.

I paused and thought. I was driving down Old Kelley Road in the rain again. I rounded the hard turn. My tires started to slide on the wet leaves. Instantly, I became more alert and compensated with the steering wheel. The car was headed for the other lane, but started to regain its right position. Halfway around the turn, headlights, bright, their high beams on. It's heading towards me!

"I can't take it anymore," I begin to sob. "I keep having nightmares about the accident. Then I can't stop thinking about the baby. Baby Samantha."

Luke sat up and wrapped me in his arms. I sobbed until my body felt like a limp strand of spaghetti held from a fork.

"Samantha is in my thoughts all the time now. I can't stop wondering if she is okay. Where is she?"

Luke stroked my arm with his fingers.

I pulled myself away and looked at him.

"I need to find her," I said firmly.

"But," he hesitated. "I thought you said that the psychiatrist said it was best to just leave her alone. She is probably fine with the aunt who adopted her."

"Yes, that was the plan years ago. I needed to focus on getting my life back together and let them do the same. But now, now my life is pretty routine." I grabbed a tissue and blew my nose.

"But don't we have enough on our hands with Amanda right now?"

My shoulders clenched. Aggravation seized my neck. "I'm sorry it's not a good time for you!" I jumped out of the bed and stood staring down at Luke.

"Jill, shhh, settle down, we're just talking about options," he patted the bare spot in the bed.

I stood firmly, not moving.

"Maybe you should call Doctor Sol and discuss this?"

"She's retired now. I don't want to bother her. Besides, isn't it time I make my own decisions? Isn't it time I take some chances even if I fall flat on my face? Isn't it time I got my shit together?" I stood straight up, pulled my head up and felt my chest puff out like a colonel awaiting salutes from his troops.

Chapter 18

AMANDA

My head slammed against the bus window when it hit the pothole on Arborvite Lane. I usually braced myself for it; I knew exactly when were going to hit it by now. But today I just didn't care. I let my head lean against it.

I felt like no one gets it. No one understands what it's like to be me. Going to "special" class, Justin doesn't even know who I am, and now, after I discovered the most amazing dolphin, it dies. And stupid Harley won't leave me alone.

My backpack sat beside me, I was hoping it would block anyone from sitting next to me. The bus stopped at the corner where a group of kids were waiting. Olivia was all chatty as usual. Her wispy bangs looked like they were just cut. Her teeth were as white as snow. She chatted away as she passed my seat; I don't exist. She headed to the back of the bus where all the cool kids hung out.

We bumped along. Ryan Cohen stood up and opened the window above his seat. The cool air blew my hair back from my face. I hated to admit it made me feel a little bit better. I sat upright and watched the leaves blow off the trees that we passed. I felt my stomach cramp as I began thinking about Saturday, the last day of the season for kayak club. I wished my parents had grounded me from that too. I didn't want to go.

Springville Middle School—the sign is painted in our school colors, red and yellow. I can't wait to go to high school. Maybe it will be better there.

The bus stopped and Mr. Goodhue got off to watch us as we marched off the bus. "Have a good day, Amanda," he smiled.

"Thanks," I mumbled and kept walking until I reached my locker where my friends were.

"So, how bad did you get it?" Kailey asked right away.

"I'm grounded from pretty much everything. They took my phone away too," I shoved my book bag in my locker and slammed the door.

Kailey looked at Rachel with her OMG face.

"For how long?" Rachel asked.

"Until Friday," I replied. As I said it, I noticed that both of their eyebrows rose in surprise. I guess they expected longer. I'm actually kinda surprised they didn't make it longer too.

"So, if you need to reach me, you'll have to try our house number. Do you know it?" I asked.

Kailey pulled her iPhone with a teal blue cover on it from her pocket. She tapped the screen until she reached me in her contacts list. "Yeah, it's in here. I think I had to give it to my mom once."

Rachel did the same and shook her head yes.

"Can you still go to the Halloween dance?"

85

"Yeah, I guess. They didn't say anything about that." Although I was not sure whether I even wanted to go now.

Rachel clapped her hands together. "Good, so are we going to go as different versions of Lady Gaga together?"

"No, I'm not doing that I told you. You two can do that."

"Aww, come on, it would be more fun with three of us." Kailey pleaded.

The bell saved me. "See you at lunch."

Chapter 19

JILL

I scurried down the hall with my purse slung over one shoulder and my briefcase, filled with my laptop and the latest nursing journals, over the other. The kids were already filtering off the buses. When I reached my office door I stood there and froze. The new keyless lock that required a punch code waited for me to enter the numbers. I stared at it... 4...41...43... *Dammit, what was the code?* I placed my finger on the button labeled four and pressed it, hoping it would just flow from there. Four click, Four what? I laid my bags down on the floor, a panicky feeling started to rise up my spine. Four, I pressed four, then three, still nothing. "Arrrrgh," I grumbled and stamped my foot.

"You need help, Nurse Cooper?" Wiley bounced up from behind me in his jubilant Gomer Pyle way.

"I am blanking out on the code, Wiley. Can you please tell me what it is?" I asked.

He replied to my request with a blank stare.

"Wiley, what's the code?" I said with a little more frustration and urgency in my voice.

Blank stare.

"Wiley, surely you saved the code somewhere, the way you keep an extra set of keys in your maintenance office for every door in this place," I looked at him sternly.

"Don't you know it? I need it now, dammit!"

He began to cower like a puppy that just peed on the rug and got caught. Without a whisper his puppy dog eyes said, "I'm sorry, I won't do it again."

"Dammit, Wiley, I'm…" I stopped, feeling multiple sets of eyes on me. I took a quick scan of the hall and indeed the children within earshot were looking and Evelyn stood at her classroom door looking at me with her head tilted.

Just then the code blurted out in my head, "Four-two-one-three."

I turned and entered the numbers before I forgot them again, and this time when I turned the doorknob it popped open. I got the same thrilling satisfaction that came when the jar top sprung open on a stubborn jar of applesauce.

The thrill instantly drained when I turned and noticed Wiley slithered away full of embarrassment. Dammit. Maybe I need to lock myself in a closet until I can get this angst out of me before I inflict more pain onto others. I had no choice but to let him go and apologize later. I was late. I gathered up my belongings and heaved them on top of my desk as someone knocked on the door.

"Jill, is everything all right?" Evelyn asked.

"I'm late," I tried.

"Yes, but you haven't been acting yourself lately. It's not like you to snap like that," she took a step closer.

I plumped down into my office chair. "I had a really bad dream last night. I think that made me wake up on the wrong side of the bed today."

Evelyn stood ready to listen to more.

"I've got some things going on, but I'm working on it. Thank you for the concern. I will apologize to Wiley after I get the first round of meds done for the kids this morning," I said dismissively. It really wasn't a good time to dump my problems out. Besides, no one at the school knew about the accident, not even Evelyn.

"Okay." She began to retreat. "But, I'm here if you need to talk. Right across the hall."

"Thanks, I appreciate that, I really do." I said sincerely as I decided it was time to put this problem to bed.

* * *

I felt obsessed as I whizzed through my morning routine. When the last child left, I closed my office door.

Maria Rodriguez Rockland Marriage I typed in the Google search box. I would start with what I last knew about them. Samantha's aunt married and moved them to New Jersey. A wedding announcement popped up in the *Rockland Times*. Maria looked beautiful, her empire waist wedding dress hugging her cellulite free body. Her hair tucked under her veil. She stood next to her groom, Juan Hernandez.

Maria and Juan Hernandez New Jersey. I knew she moved to New Jersey after they married, but I wasn't sure what part.

A list of 15 varying combinations of people with these names popped up on the screen.

Samantha Hernandez New Jersey. Bingo! A picture of five

girls wearing Girl Scouts uniforms stood around a group of elderly people. *Local Girl Scout troop brings cheer to Rocky Mount Nursing Home Residents.* Samantha's name was listed amongst the girls. I leaned back in my chair and stared at her image. The tallest of the girls, she had straight, jet-black hair and dark, kind eyes. The bright smile on her face was like seeing the North Star on a clear dark night. Then a twinge of doubt snuck in my head. Maybe she is fine. She looks fine. Maybe I should just leave her alone. What if I interrupt her life? What if she doesn't want to see me? What if I make her relive all the pain I've felt all these years?

My eyes scoured the picture over and over. 2008. The picture was taken in 2008, when Samantha was 13 years old. But where was she now?

I heard a tiny knock on my door. It opened before I could get to it.

"Nurse Cooper, I don't feel good."

Toby Maron stood with his hands to his side, his face flush and nose sniffling.

I clicked the screen closed and asked, "What's not feeling good, Toby?"

* * *

Lately I had been just chomping on nuts in my office, because I was too busy to make it to lunch in the teacher's lounge. I made it a point to get there today. As I entered, Antonio was stealing the show once again.

When he saw me he proclaimed, "I don't know how you do it!" Before I could ask what he was referencing to, he continued on. "Every day it gets worse. Snot running out of their noses. At first it was just a few of them, but now it seems like it's growing. They wipe it all over their sleeves or just let it run down their faces." His hands danced in the air. "I tell them, blow your nose in a tissue. You know what some of them tell me? 'I need you to hold it for me, Mr. Suarez.'" He pretended to gag. "I think I'm going to be sick."

I could hear snickering from around the room. "It's the beginning of flu season, unfortunately, it happens," I tried to offer some compassion, while I contemplated telling him this was only the beginning.

"I cannot do this; some of them even have green snot coming out. I will need to call you to help me." He started to look green himself.

Those within earshot, collectively cowered and cried, "Eww."

"Antonio, we're trying to eat," Evelyn said, holding her hand up to him.

"I'm sorry, Antonio, but I can't come and help you with kids who need to clean up their noses. If something's out of the ordinary, by all means send them to my office. Maybe you should ask Mr. Peterson if he can hire someone to wipe noses. And butts, we need that too." I meant it as a joke, but he took it as a possibility.

"That might work, I will talk to him." He paused, then added, "*Ayy yi yi*, what am I going to do? My fiancée wants lots of kids." He combed his hair with his fingers.

I softened. "Antonio, trust me, when they're your own, you'll be able to do things you never thought possible. Love will enable you."

* * *

Anxious to get home and continue searching for Samantha, I marched down the hall toward the front door. Mr. Peterson, our school principal, closed his office door and walked in my direction. As we passed each other, he gave me a thumbs up and smiled. "Good one."

It took me a second to figure out what he was referencing to, then I stopped and turned as he kept walking. "He actually came and asked you?"

"I listened. Then I handed him a box of tissues." With that, he turned his head away and continued down the hall.

Chapter 20

AMANDA

"How was school today?" Mom asked from the computer desk in the kitchen.

"Okay," I moaned, then headed for the fridge in search of a snack. Mom didn't badger me for more information. She turned back at the computer screen and kept plucking away.

"So, what do you think?" Sarah said as she came in the kitchen holding up a green and teal blue sequined mermaid tail. She didn't wait for us to respond. "I'm going to attach it to my aqua body suit and add big clam shells." She put her hands over her boobs and threw her hair back.

"It's beautiful," Mom said, turning away from the computer. "You did a perfect job with the seams on the side; I don't even see the stitches."

Sarah beamed.

I just mumbled, "Nice." What I really wanted to say was, *Will you make me one?* I bet that would get Justin's attention. Sewing is not my thing. I tried getting into it. Mom and Sarah loved to make clothes and stuff. My lines never came out straight. I couldn't even make a square pillow look square.

"I'm not sure what color to paint my hair, what do you think?"

Mom was back leaning into the computer screen.

"Whatever you think, honey," she mumbled.

I shrugged my shoulders.

My sister skipped away and headed back upstairs.

I took the last chocolate pudding cup, peeled the top off and tossed it in the recycling bin. I shuffled through the silverware drawer to find a small spoon and sat down at the kitchen table. Mom sat staring at the screen reading something as I licked the spoon clean.

Her silence was getting weird. "What are you looking at?" I asked.

She kept reading.

Scraping the last morsel of pudding off the side of the container with my finger, I got out of my chair. I went over and stood behind her. She didn't flinch.

A Facebook page filled the screen. A pretty girl with dark hair sat on a bike. Samantha Hernandez.

"Who's Samantha Hernandez?" I asked.

Startled, Mom clicked the page closed. "No one."

"What do you mean 'no one'? You were sitting there staring."

"Do you want a snack?" she asked as she stood up.

"Just had one. Who is that girl?" The more Mom acted like she didn't want me to know, the more I wanted to know.

"What girl?" Sarah asked as she returned to the kitchen.

"No one," Mom tried again. "What do you want for

dinner?"

"Mom was reading the Facebook page of some girl named Samantha," I told my sister.

"That's kinda creepy, Mom. Do you know her?"

"It's a long story," Mom began to cave. She pulled a bag of potatoes out of the fridge and began to wash them.

"We're listening," Sarah stood, her arms crossed.

I crossed mine too.

Mom put the potato peeler down and turned to us. Her face looked serious. Maybe we don't want to know who that girl is.

"Why don't we wait for your dad to get home? Then I'll explain."

Chapter 21

JILL

I wasn't planning on telling the girls. I needed time to think. "Go and start your homework. I'll call you when your father gets home."

"But—" they both started to say.

"I said, go upstairs and start your homework." I pointed towards the door. Reluctantly, they left.

The skin on the potato practically scrubbed right off I was rubbing it so hard. I washed off three more, then put them on the cutting board and stabbed holes in them. Where do I start? How much do I tell them? For a fleeting moment I thought about conjuring up a different story. No, lying to them will only erode their trust. I was still trying to figure all this out for myself. Now I need to factor in my daughters' thoughts and reactions. My hand reached out and held the counter as if it could help steady me. My eyes searched out the window for answers. It was all so long ago. Maybe I should have just left it alone.

Luke's car door slammed outside and the girls trampled down the upstairs hallway toward the stairs. It was all coming at me too fast. I'm starting to feel like I couldn't breathe. The backdoor knob jiggled. The girls ran into the kitchen. Luke gave the door a strong push. He stopped when he saw my face.

"Dad, who's Samantha?" the girls chimed in unison.

Luke immediately stared at me.

"I have to tell them," was all I could squeak out.

Chapter 22

AMANDA

"Wait, so you killed her parents?" Sarah asked. She didn't dare stand up. Dad told us we had to all sit around the table and talk about this like adults. I wasn't exactly sure what that meant, but I figured it meant we couldn't be too dramatic.

"No, Sarah, it was an accident," Dad said firmly. Mom bit her lip. It was beginning to wiggle.

"But, both of the baby's parents died?" Sarah fired. "Who took care of the baby?"

"The baby's aunt." Dad answered.

"Why didn't you tell us?" Sarah asked. She was asking all the questions I had in my head, so I let her go ahead. My eyes followed the conversation like a volleyball.

"Honey, it all happened before you were born," Mom said. She placed her hands on the table and held them together.

"So, why do you want to find her now? Why can't we just leave her alone?" Sarah's voice got more scared.

Dad looked at Mom. I guess he didn't know the answer. She took a deep breath.

"This isn't a 'we' decision. This is something that I need to do," Mom was getting aggravated. She always started clenching her jaw and trying to stretch her neck at the same time when she got this way.

"But what if she doesn't want you to find her?"

What if we don't want you to look for her is what I wanted to say.

"I don't expect you to understand, but this is something that has been haunting me for a long time. I need to see her for myself. I need to know that she is okay." Mom said, then added, "And I need you to keep this in the family for right now. I don't want you talking to anyone about this. Not your friends, not your grandparents, just us. Is that clear?"

I nodded my head. Dad turned and looked at Sarah who was having a stare down with Mom.

Sarah just said sarcastically, "Great." Then leaned back in a huff.

Friday couldn't come soon enough, I thought.

Chapter 23

JILL

"You may as well stay up and watch the *Tonight Show* with me," Luke joked as he sat on the couch, feet up on the coffee table, diving into a popcorn bowl fist by fist.

"I'm afraid to go to sleep." I say as I plopped down next to him.

"Popcorn?" he offered the bowl.

"No, thanks," I said and let my head, with its suitcase packed with troubles, rest on his shoulder.

"Ya know, I've been thinking. I had a client who was adopted. She used a private detective to find her birth parents. Local guy. He is a retired cop. I could get his name for you," he finished what was in his mouth and waited for an answer from me before continuing his dive to the bottom of the bowl.

My head rose, feeling a bit lighter. "Really?" I said. "Because honestly, I'm stuck. The trail on the Internet is dead. I can't figure out where she is now. She doesn't seem to be where they moved to in New Jersey years ago."

"I'll make some calls tomorrow and get you this guy's number. Jill, I think it will be better to have a professional help you with this."

I hugged my husband while he clung to his popcorn bowl with one hand and reached around me with the other. "You have no idea how much your support means to me. I feel like I have been carrying around a backpack full of rocks for years. Each year, I swear someone puts a bigger boulder in it."

Luke sat still and let me talk. He is so good at that. *How did I get so lucky*, I wondered.

"It's just mind boggling. The whole thing. I don't even know how to explain it to you. You wake up one day, go about your business and BOOM! In a sheer instant your world is changed forever. And Samantha's world was changed forever. And her family's world is changed forever. And even my family, who were forced to bear the trauma with me—changed forever. No matter how much I try to figure it out or get over it, I can't. It actually makes my head hurt."

"I can't imagine," Luke leaned over and put the popcorn bowl on the coffee table. He hugged me like he would never let me go. He stroked my hair. I let his compassion soak into my soul even though I didn't feel like I deserved it. I needed it. "Well, we'll just have to find this young lady," his tone hopeful.

I nodded my head but said nothing. *And what if finding her doesn't help*, I wondered. No, I can't even think about that, because then I'm out of options.

Chapter 24

AMANDA

"Can you pass me that test tube?" Alice Wong, my science lab partner asked. The safety goggles only came in one size. It was all I could do not to laugh when I looked at her wearing them on her tiny head. She may as well have been going scuba diving.

I passed her the test tube with blue in it. "This one?"

"Yeah." She took it from me and added it to the clear liquid sitting in a petri dish in front of her. It began to fizz.

I didn't really like science, but I liked being in a regular class. What made me excited about going to science class was Justin. When it came time to pick lab partners, I willed with all my might for him to come and pick me but Tyler Radison asked him, "Dude, want to be partners?"

Justin shrugged his shoulders and said, "Sure."

My BFFs were not in my class so I began frantically looking around the room. Partners paired up mostly by who was standing next to each other. Before I knew it I was down to Alice Wong or David.

"Looks like it's you and me," Alice said as if she couldn't care less who her partner was.

I shook my head yes. At least she was smart. I could use a good grade in this class.

As Alice leaned over and watched the concoction bubble and steamy gas rise from the top, I snuck a glance at Justin on the other side of the long black table. The sink in the middle was in my way, so I leaned forward to get a better view.

Justin and Tyler were joking around. Justin's smile, his perfect teeth, his blond hair still with streaks of sun from the summer made me woozy.

"I think it's working," Alice announced as if she just discovered electricity. My bubble popped and I returned to our project. Not before sneaking one more peek at the boy that I wanted to call mine.

"Are you going to the Halloween dance next week?" she asked as she jotted notes down on the pad we shared.

"Not sure yet," I answered. I really didn't want to get into it. "You?"

"Yeah, I can't wait. I have a cool costume. I'm not telling anyone yet what it is though. I really want to win the costume contest."

I didn't care about winning a costume contest. I had my own prize in mind. FOMO was beginning to set in. Fear of Missing Out. Maybe I should go to the dance. If only I could get my sister to make me a really cool costume like hers.

Chapter 25

JILL

Tony Figarone sat across the small table for two at Starbucks. "Yeah, I remember that case. Tragic." He shook his head.

He was pretty much what I expected, but kinder and warmer. He was a big, heavyset guy who ate too many donuts in his time. He sipped his cup and looked like he went back to 1995 in his mind.

I was instantly relieved. I didn't have to explain what happened. Didn't have to relive it for the umpteenth time. "This is as far as I can find her on the Internet," I handed him printouts of the article that I found and her Facebook page, which was highly protected. She must be a smart girl.

He looked at the image. I pointed to Samantha.

Tony eyed the photograph. Took another sip of his coffee. "But this is back in 2008."

He was quick. A spring of hope erupted inside of me.

"Have you thought about what you are going to do if I find her?" He put the photograph down on the table and maintained eye contact with me.

I was embarrassed to share my ideas with him. Ring her

doorbell with a big bouquet of flowers and beg her forgiveness? Stalk her until I find a moment that feels right? I hadn't really thought that far or about the potential repercussions. "Do you have any suggestions? What do people in my position usually do?"

"Whatever you do, don't surprise her. This type of thing is big. It needs to be handled delicately." He let his coffee cup rest on the table and leaned closer to me. "When I find her, I will get you her address. I suggest you write this Samantha a letter, but mail it addressed to her aunt. She's still a minor at seventeen. It will be up to her aunt whether she feels Samantha is able to handle this."

Immediately I noticed the change of words from if to when I find her. This is really going to happen. I could feel it in my gut, which was churning with excitement and a huge dose of jitters.

Chapter 26

AMANDA

Rachel Text: *Cool, you got your phone back!*

Me Text: *Yeah, it sucked without it.*

Rachel Text: *It's supposed to rain tomorrow. Do you think we'll get to go to our last kayak session?*

Me Text: *Not sure.* I was hoping it would pour. I didn't want to go and I didn't want to have to explain why. I was getting tired of my parents pretending like they were looking for something. I knew they kept coming into the room that I was in to check on me.

Rachel Text: *Kailey and I have decided to go as Lady Gaga. You don't have much time to come up with a costume. The dance is next Wednesday, ya know.*

Me Text: *I'm gonna go.* As what, I didn't know. I would have to come up with something this weekend.

Rachel Text: *Yay!*

Mom said, "Dinner is almost ready!"

Me Text: *Gotta go.*

Rachel Text: *See ya.*

Chapter 27

JILL

It was the perfect day to sleep in. Rain battered down on the roof and spattered across the windows. I didn't even bother waking up Amanda for her last day of kayaking. I could only hope that she would continue it next year; she seemed to really enjoy it.

By 10:00 a.m., I decided I had better get up. Sarah left a note that she went to cheer at the football game. Luke left a note, *went into the office to get some last minute tax work done.* He promised to be home at lunch.

I found myself with an unusual need to sort through clutter and organize it. I went up to my bedroom closet. It smelled of cedar. I pushed aside a row of dresses to expose a few shoeboxes below. Rarely was there an occasion these days to wear my high heeled patent leather shoes or the "work it, own it" pumps I wore years ago when we were newly married. For some reason I kept them. Maybe I'll wear them again, I told myself. I picked those boxes up and placed them on the floor beside me as I sat down cross-legged. On the very bottom of the pile was what I was looking for.

A shoebox not much different from the others lay before me. I reached over and placed the shiny white box with black letters on the top on my lap. My hand circled the top before I opened it. Inside was a pile of cards. One by one I opened them and read what was handwritten inside. "Happy Birthday, we love you! Love, Mom and Dad,"; "Congratulations, we are so proud of you! Love, Mom and Dad." I wondered if Dad even knew Mom bought the cards. Years worth of love, reduced to a shoebox. At the very bottom were two newspaper clippings.

Local family killed, baby survives. Unthinkable Tragedy. I re-read the headlines. I held them in front of me, a reminder that the nightmare was indeed real.

I really hoped that Tony would find Samantha quickly. He declined to give me a time estimate. "I just don't know. Sometimes a couple of days, sometimes years, sometimes-" he stopped. He didn't need to tell me sometimes he doesn't find them. "She's local though. That's a positive."

I packed the treasures back into their box and stored them away. Placed the shoes that were drifting away from the possibility of being worn on top. Then I remembered the doll. The one my mother made me. Using a hanger, I reached up to the top shelf and pulled down a plastic bag. As it dropped, I caught it. I untied the knot and found Heidi as I had left her many years ago. Heidi, I had named her when I was a little girl. For the life of me, I don't know why I picked that name. She was supposed to look like me, gold hair, green eyes and she wore a pink dress. I would put her in the den.

As I stood up, I heard the kitchen door slam. Who

could that be?

I climbed down the stairs like a cat looking for prey. Peaches snored away on the couch. I heard the kitchen pantry door open and someone rummaging inside. As I peered into the doorway, Sarah came out of the pantry, stuffing Ritz crackers in her mouth with the box still in her hand. Her hair was matted to her head from the rain. Mascara smudged under her eyes. She acted like I wasn't there, although I stood just a few feet away from her.

"What are you doing home so early?" I asked.

She stuffed more crackers in her mouth as she headed for the refrigerator. "I was hungry," she said between chews.

I watched inquisitively. As she eyed the choices in the fridge, her shoulders started to shake. Then I heard giggling.

"What's so funny?" I asked.

Her giggles grew into laughter. She threw her hand over her mouth as bits of cracker spurt out.

As I began to inch closer to her, Luke came through the kitchen door.

"What's for lunch, I'm starving," he said unfazed. But even he picked up quickly that something was not right. It must have been the look I shot him.

"Look at how the pickles are sitting next to the jelly," Sarah giggled and looked at Luke.

His eyebrows furrowed, then released. He looked at me, then back at Sarah. He walked right up to her, reached his hand out and grabbed her by the jaw. He turned her face toward his and stared at her. "Are you high?"

"High?" she murmured through her cheeks that were squashed between Luke's fingers. Her body waved like seaweed swaying on the bottom of the ocean floor.

"Yes, high," he said louder and let her go.

"What the—" I started. Luke held up his stop-I'm-handling-this hand.

He ripped the box of crackers away from her and pointed towards the door. "Go upstairs and sleep it off. There's no use discussing this while you're in this state."

She reached to get the crackers back. He held them behind his back. "I said go, NOW!!"

Sarah sauntered out of the kitchen like a groovy hippie chick. As she reached the stairs she tossed back, "You're so uncool."

"What's going on?" My life was starting to feel like a big game of whack-a-mole. Just when I started to get one problem under control, another reared its ugly head out.

"I don't know," he pushed the hair away from his forehead. "This isn't like her."

I had to agree. Our biggest problem with Sarah was her lack of self-esteem.

Chapter 28

AMANDA

I don't know why I had to be the one to get Sarah for dinner. I crept up to her door and knocked twice, lightly. No answer. I stood there and waited but still no answer. Slowly I turned the doorknob and peeked my head in. Sarah was lying in bed with a pillow over her head, only her nose and mouth showing.

"Sarah," I whispered carefully. There was no knowing what kind of dragon I could be waking.

Her hand raised, she pulled the pillow up to expose her eyes in the darkness underneath. "What?"

"Mom and Dad want you to come down for dinner."

She let the pillow fall back over her face. I looked around her room. The picture of her and Alex that used to sit on her desk was lying face down on the floor. Her mermaid tail sparkling with sequins slung over her desk chair. I went over and let my fingers run across the shimmer.

"You can have it," she growled as she sat up. Her hair was all knotted. She looked worse than when she was barfing all day with the flu last winter.

I looked at her, my head tilted.

"I said you can have it," she turned and looked out the window.

"But—" I started.

"Alex broke up with me. I'm not going to the Halloween dance," she stood up now and looked in the mirror. She opened a jar of makeup remover and began to remove the dark smudges under her eyes.

I stifled the excitement inside. "Why?"

"I don't know," she rubbed the pad harder on her face. "He's taking Emma Lasdon instead. Can you believe it?"

"That sucks," I said. *But it doesn't suck for me. I get the mermaid costume and I don't even have to trade it to do your chores*, I thought to myself. I would wait to celebrate later in the privacy of my own room.

"Yeah," she turned to me. "Are they pissed?"

"I think so. But from what I can hear I think they are more confused why you did this. Have you been doing it a long time?" I asked.

Sarah took a ponytail holder off her bureau and gathered the clump of mess on her head, which was normally neatly combed, into it. "No, it was my first time. Gabby on my cheerleading team told me it would make me feel better after Alex broke up with me this morning."

"Girls!" Mom yelled from the bottom of the stairs.

I let Sarah lead the way.

* * *

"We don't understand. What were you thinking?" Dad lit

112

into Sarah as soon as she hit the kitchen.

My stomach was so nervous for her. My appetite was completely ruined. How many times did they lecture us about not doing drugs?

Sarah picked up her napkin and put it on her lap. She didn't take her eyes off it as she said with attitude, "I'm sorry."

"Sorry? What in the world would make you take drugs?" Dad wasn't going to let this one go. I could tell. Everyone was at the table now and all eyes were on Sarah. The lasagna sat in the center steaming. No one touched it.

Sarah sat silent. Her head looked like it was sinking further down towards her chest. The tension in the room made me fidget in my chair. Where was Peaches when you needed her? Finally I couldn't take it anymore.

"Alex broke up with her," I tattled.

Mom and Dad looked at each other. Dad's face softened.

"Is that true?" Mom asked as she reached out and placed her hand on Sarah's shoulder.

"Yeah, he broke up with me this morning. I'm sorry. I won't do it again. I only tried it this once," she looked at Mom.

Dad flopped back in his chair and looked up to the ceiling and mouthed, "Thank you, God." Sarah didn't see him. He parted his lips; his shoulders sank away from his head. "Miss one bus, catch the next. Sarah, there will be plenty of guys who want to go out with you. You don't have to worry about that." He reached and lifted a big chunk of lasagna from the pan. The mozzarella cheese oozed down the sides of the spatula and left a trail all the way to his plate.

"I'm sorry, honey," Mom took the spatula from Dad and served us each a piece, then herself. "Your dad is right. In fact, maybe you want to explore having some time for yourself."

Sarah just shrugged her shoulders and began to pick at a corner of her pasta.

"Sarah said I can have her mermaid costume," I said, desperate to change the subject.

"You're not going to the dance?" Mom asked sadly.

"No."

"Will you help me fit it to my size?" I asked them.

"Sure," Sarah said. She was being surprisingly extra nice to me. I took it while I could get it. Wait until Rachel and Kailey see it!

Chapter 29

JILL

It took Tony exactly five days, three hours and forty-three minutes to find Samantha. Just in the nick of time. There was not a sock drawer, linen closet or kitchen cupboard that wasn't purged, scrubbed and neatly organized in my house.

"I found her. She lives in Indian Valley," he sounded a bit out of breath on the other side of the phone.

"Indian Valley? That's just twenty minutes from here."

"Yeah, her aunt/mother, whatever you want to call her divorced that guy she married. Guess he was beating her. She got a restraining order two years ago and moved back to Indian Valley." The sound of a can cracked open in the background. "Have you thought about how you're going to approach them?"

"I'm going to take your suggestion and write a letter, but mail it to her aunt/mom, Maria." I wondered how Samantha referred to her. I wondered if they got along.

"Good, I'm glad. I'm going to text you their address when I get off the phone," Tony said just like that. Like this was an everyday thing. For him maybe yes, me absolutely not. I felt a sudden urge to run to the bathroom.

"Okay." I didn't know what else to say.

"Hey, good luck. Let me know how it all works out, will ya?"

Chapter 30

AMANDA

I practiced how to walk all week in my mermaid tail while I imagined swimming in the sea with dolphins around me. Fast, then slow, then jumping high out of the ocean! Maybe mermaids are real? Wouldn't that be cool? If I really were a mermaid, I could help get all of the plastic out of the ocean.

Rachel and Kailey waited outside the front door of the school as planned. Rachel wore a dress covered with Kermit the Frog puppets, including one pinned to her white-blond wig like a flower. Her wig was cut into a bob with bangs. Her eyes were caked with mascara. She wore green tights and green flats. I think Lady Gaga would have worn funkier shoes, but I didn't say anything. Kailey was plastered with clear blue balloons from her shoulders down to just above her knees. She wore black tights sprinkled with glitter and platform black shoes. The wig seemed the same as the one Rachel wore, except Kailey's was left long and had a stripe of yellow in it.

"So glad you guys didn't opt for the meat dress or the egg," I said as I stood back and admired their creativity. "They actually came out pretty cool."

They smiled and gave each other a high five.

"Go ahead, turn around let us see," Kailey waved her finger in a circle.

I turned slowly, my hands in the air so they could see all the sequins sparkle.

Rachel nodded her head, "Nice!"

Kailey added, "Sweet!"

"Ready to go in?" Rachel asked.

We followed her behind someone dressed in a giant bear costume. The hallways were all blocked off only allowing us to go to the gym or the bathrooms right next to it. The music was playing really loud. The room was already full; we definitely were "fashionably late" as my mother would say.

"There's Max," Kailey whispered to us. "Over there, he's dressed like a cop."

"Isn't his dad a cop?" I asked.

"I think so," Kailey replied as she stared.

"That's kinda lame, don't you think for a costume?"

Kailey didn't seem to care in the slightest. I looked around for Justin. I had no idea what he was dressed as. After the third scan around the room, I began to wonder if coming here was a bad idea.

"Let's go get a soda or something," Rachel waved us to follow her to the refreshments table. As we waited; I heard that voice behind me.

"Cool costume, Cooper. Are you going home to the ocean after this to swim with your dolphin friends?"

My teeth clenched. Harley. Before I could turn around, I heard another voice say, "Hey, why don't you just leave her alone?"

My head whipped around and Superman himself was looking down at Harley. His hair slicked back and dyed black, with a big S on his chest and even the blue tights with red boots.

"I'm just jokin' with her," Harley's hand pushed Superman's hand off his shoulder. Harley stepped out of line and walked away.

"Wow, thanks, Justin," I gushed. My cheeks got warm and my mouth was dying for a soda.

"I heard about the dolphin thing. That sucks," he said.

Justin Powell. I'm standing here talking to Justin Powell. I froze. I could hear Kailey and Rachel snickering behind me. They moved forward in the line without me.

"Yeah," was the only thing that came to mind.

An awkward silence sat between us. Maroon 5's "One More Night" came on. Justin turned and looked at the dance floor. "You wanna dance?"

Suddenly I wasn't thirsty.

We walked to the dance floor. My hands got really sweaty. I didn't practice dancing in my tail! I never really believed Justin would notice me. Talk to me. Dance with me!

He was smooth. We rocked back and forth, he looked away and then back at me and smiled. The dimple in his cheek made me want to melt into the floor. I swayed back and forth. Occasionally, I tossed my long glittering blue hair behind my back. Not because it was bothering me in the front, just because I didn't really know what to do with my hands.

When the song ended, he touched my arm and I almost passed out. We headed back to the refreshment table and he grabbed a Coke, I got a Sprite, just in case I spilled it.

"That's a really cool costume," he stood back and admired.

"Thanks," I beamed. "My mom and sister made it."

"Really? I bought mine." He took a sip of his soda.

"Yours is cool too," I complimented him. I really wanted to say "you look smoking hot in it," but I didn't dare venture that far.

"Your costume is amazing!" Alice said.

I didn't recognize her at first.

"You might actually win the contest."

"Thanks, Alice. Yours is really cool too." I kept the conversation short. I didn't want Justin to walk away. I knew I should introduce them, but I didn't.

"See ya," she got the hint and headed towards the dance floor.

On the other side of the room I saw Kailey and Rachel talking to Max. Kailey spotted me eyeing them and gave me a secret thumbs up.

A slow song came on. "As Long As You Love Me." I rubbed my cup of soda back and forth in my hand. Justin reached over and took it from me and put it on a nearby table. "Shall we?"

Is this magic fairy dust in my hair? I could hardly breathe as I felt Justin walking behind me. When we reached the dance floor I turned, slowly, unsure. I've never done slow dancing before. I did what the other girls were doing. Reached up and put my arms on his shoulders, while he placed his hands on my hips. No body touching. That was part of the rules. We wandered in circles for what felt like forever. I would have been perfectly happy if it really was forever.

As the music lowered, Mr. Muccio's voice shouted at us along with the screech of his microphone. The gym lights got brighter. We all turned and looked at him onstage.

"Okay, we are getting ready for the costume parade. I want you to separate into a boys' line and a girls' line. Both lines are going to walk by the stage and take a moment to circle and show the judges your costumes. The judges this year are Mrs. Henderson, everyone's favorite art teacher; Mrs. Farraro, everyone's favorite gym teacher, and Mr. Glover, everyone's favorite custodian. Let's give them a round of applause!"

Everyone clapped.

"The prizes this year are," he reached behind him and picked up an iPad, "for first place, an iPad. For second place, an iTunes gift card worth $25 and for third place a $10 gift certificate to Trugoys. Go ahead now and get into the two lines."

Justin and I tapped each other on the hand.

"Good luck, see ya later."

I just smiled. I had nothing to say. I wasn't even sure I was still on this planet.

Chapter 31

JILL

Dear Samantha,

I sat, pen in hand, poised to write, but stupefied on what to say. I didn't want to shock her. I did want her to know that her parents weren't killed by some crazy person that didn't care. I didn't want to dump all the weight, the burden of guilt and despair that I've been carrying into her lap. If I really looked inside myself, what I wanted was for her to forgive me. Oh God, please tell me what to say.

I sat back. Stared at the fancy Crane & Co. stationery with a bumblebee emblem on top that I bought especially for this letter. The refrigerator hummed its tune. I thought this would flow out of me. My elbow rested on the table, while my fingers tried to rub an idea into my head. Nothing. I felt paralyzed.

After a half hour, I realized this couldn't be forced. I picked up the sheet of expensive stationery, tore it in shreds and threw it in the recycling bin.

Chapter 32

AMANDA

"You should have won," Alice said as she scoured through our environmental science textbook. She pulled her goggles off her eyes and slid them to rest on the top of her head like a headband. "Your costume was so much better than Sylvia's."

"Thanks," I really wanted to change the subject. When they announced that Mr. Glover was one of the judges, I knew I didn't have a chance at winning first prize. I couldn't blame him for not picking me. Besides, I got Justin's attention. That was worth more to me than an iPad.

Alice laid her calculator in the middle of the open pages like a bookmark.

"Do you want me to hold it open for you?" I offered.

"Nah, this will work."

"Everyone," Mr. Harris called to the class with his hands around his mouth like a megaphone. "Stop what you're doing for a minute."

We all stopped and looked his way.

He headed for the blackboard and began to write. "Eighth Grade Science Fair. Next week." He laid the chalk at the bottom of the board and wiped the dust off on the side of his pants. "I need you to pick a partner. A different person than who you are already partners with. Each pair will pick a topic that you will do a poster presentation on. The topic must be environmentally related."

Immediately I turned my head to Justin and he did the same back to me. Justin pointed at me, and then back at himself, his head tilted slightly down with his eyebrows raised suggestively. I nodded back enthusiastically. *Yes*, I thought to myself.

"You will each get a 3 foot by 6 foot table to display your topic. The fair will be held in the gym and all of the middle school will visit your displays after their lunch period. Any questions?" He leaned back against the chalkboard.

"So, acid rain is environmental, right?" Todd asked.

"Yes, you could choose that as your topic if you like. Oh, and everyone has to choose a different topic, no duplicates. He pulled a yellow lined pad out of his desk drawer and picked up a pen. "I am going to leave this on my desk. I want you to write your names down and your topic."

The room bustled as everyone chose new partners. Justin came right over to me. "Got any ideas for a topic?"

"Plastic's deadly effect on marine life," I said. For once I was actually excited to do something in this science class.

"Okay," Justin said. "Better go write it down."

Chapter 33

JILL

The more I tried to write the letter, the less it said what I was feeling. I was reluctant to ask for help and ideas. I wanted it to be authentic, from the heart. My heart.

I fumbled around the empty kitchen. The tea canister was empty. As I foraged through the cupboard looking for tea bags, I stumbled upon some cans of pureed pumpkin. To the right of them, a half opened bag of flour. Before I knew it, I pulled all the ingredients out to make my mother's famous homemade pumpkin bread. All I needed were a couple of the fresh eggs that I collected this morning.

Flour, sugar, baking soda, baking powder, a touch of salt, oil, vanilla extract, cinnamon and finally the pumpkin and it was ready to be stirred. The batter swirled around and around in the bowl sticking to the wooden spoon I held. Lost in the mesmerizing task, the letter came to me.

I dropped the spoon in the bowl and grabbed a piece of junk mail out of the recycle bucket. On the back of a credit card solicitation letter I jotted the letter down quickly then stepped back and read it over.

Dear Samantha,

My name is Jill Cooper, formerly Jill Bradley. If the name is not familiar to you, I am the person who was involved in the accident that took away your parents. My greatest hope is that this letter will not hurt you. I only mean to offer you a chance to talk about it, if you want to.

I need you to know that although the accident was many years ago, I think of you and your family all the time. You are in my prayers every day. I also pray for your parents' souls.

If you would ever like to meet, please do not hesitate to contact me. If not, that is okay too. As I said, I do not mean to disrupt your life. But please know, that I deeply share the grief of their loss.

Is it too much about me, and my needs? I wondered. Does it convey the enormity of pain I bear without dumping that weight on her? I read it twice more. Then, before I changed my mind, before I tore it up like the others, I ran upstairs and got a stamp from Luke's desk. I transcribed the letter on the nice stationery, addressed it to her aunt, and sealed the envelope after remembering to add a separate piece of paper with my contact information on it. As I peeled the stamp and placed it on the top right corner of the envelope, I felt a sense of peace wash over me.

Chapter 34

AMANDA

"Do you want to come over to my house after school?" Rachel asked. "Kailey is coming."

"Can't, I'm going to work with Justin on our science fair project." I exchanged books for our last period class, math, boring.

"So, now that you have a boyfriend, you don't hang out with your friends anymore?" she tilted her hip and put her hand on it waiting for an answer.

Justin finally knows who I am and now I have to deal with this from someone who says she's my friend? I never gave her flack when she was hanging out with Roger. I didn't even tell anyone that they kissed when she made me swear not too. Besides, I don't know if Justin is really my boyfriend.

"It's worth half our grade," I defended myself. If it weren't for Alice, the other half of my grade would be an F. Even Mr. Harris knew that.

"Well, how about tomorrow?" she held her stance, determined to make me commit to hanging out with her.

"I'll ask my mom," I said, trying to come up with an

excuse until I could see if Justin wanted to do something. Luckily, Rachel bought it, and let me off the hook for now.

* * *

Justin was waiting for me in the back corner of the library at a big table by the window. We sat next to each other and put the pieces of information into piles that we would later group onto boards together.

"Scary, if we keep using plastic, we are going to be buried in it," Justin said. "I have to admit, I never really thought about it before."

He stood up and leaned over in front of me to put the plastic bottle cards on the "types of plastic" pile. He smelled good, really good, kinda like my dad but fresher, like spearmint gum. It made my legs wobble, I was so glad I wasn't standing. As he sat back down his smell drifted by me again.

I handed him a pile of pictures of all the marine animals that were dying from eating plastic: dolphins, whales, turtles, seabirds. He flipped through them and stopped at the one with hundreds of dead birds lying on a beach.

"Sad," he whispered.

"Yeah," I agreed. "My dad said they didn't have this problem when he was young. He says they didn't have plastic bottles. He calls bottled water the newest pet rock."

"Pet rock?"

"I guess they used to sell rocks as pets," I shrugged. "It was a big thing years ago. You have to remember, my dad didn't have electricity either," I mocked.

Justin laughed. "My parents are from the dinosaur age, too. 'We had water fountains and if you were thirsty, you just had to wait until you got to one,' " Justin made a fist and swung it in the air in front of him.

I laughed. My phone bleeped with a text.

"Where are you?" my mother.

"Be right out, just finishing," I typed back. "My mom is here," I told Justin as I began to gather the different piles and putting them in separate folders.

Justin gave me a hand and asked, "Do you want to come to my house after school tomorrow so we can paste all these on the boards?" Before I could answer, he quickly added, "That way they can dry, we won't have to move them. I can have my mom drop them off the day of the fair. I live just two blocks from here. We can walk."

I knew exactly where he lived. I Googled everything about him long before I met him. He lived on Sullivan Street where the old Victorian houses that my mother always admires are.

"Sure, that sounds like a good idea," I said excitedly, hoping my mother would say yes.

I lined the folders up carefully in my book bag, leaving Justin standing there. "See ya tomorrow!"

Chapter 35

JILL

She must have received the letter by now, I thought on the way into work. Only the red maples clung to their bright red leaves now. The other trees had all shed theirs and they danced along the roadside. Maybe I should have waited until after the New Year to send her the letter, the holidays are so busy. And stressful.

I peeled the pumpkins and ghosts off my office window and put up turkeys and pilgrim hats. November already. Just a few more weeks and we'll be sitting on the warm tropical Triton beach. I felt more connected just thinking about it. It was hard to tell who in our family needed the vacation most. *If we all come back in a better state of mind, it will be well worth it*, I decided.

The sound of a child wailing reached my office door before Toby did.

Marilyn, one of the school monitors explained, "He got hit in the head with a kickball."

Toby held his hand on his forehead, right where his thick curly brown hair met the skin. I squatted down before him and gently pulled his hand away. "Good thing it was a kickball and not a bowling ball!"

Toby nodded his head in agreement, like that was a possible alternative, his crying now turned to sniffling. Marilyn tried not to laugh. Sometimes these kids were just so darned cute.

There was barely a red spot. "Toby, how about you lie down on my special cot and I will put an ice pack on it. After a few minutes, you'll be good as new."

He nodded again, headed for the cot as I excused Marilyn with a thumbs-up. *If I were smart I would invest my retirement funds in the company that makes these instant ice packs,* I thought as I smashed it into action and placed it on his head.

Next up, Keisha.

"My belly hurts," she whined and rubbed her stomach. Her pants had a hole over her knee and her sweater had stains down the front.

"Come on in, Keisha, and have a seat next to my desk." I grabbed my thermometer and sat next to her.

"Are you having any problem going to the bathroom?"

She shook her head no.

"Have you thrown up?"

Another no.

I placed the thermometer in her ear and reached over for my stethoscope.

"That's good, 98.9. I'm going to lift your sweater just a little and listen to your belly, okay?"

She nodded yes with skepticism and looked down to watch what I was doing.

"Hmmm ..." I said. Hmmm, overactive bowel sounds.

"I hear a lion roaring in there!" I let her sweater fall back down and looked at her. Keeping my tone light, I asked, "What did you have for breakfast?"

"I didn't have breakfast," she squirmed.

Just as I suspected.

Mr. Peterson keeps telling me he's working on this issue.

Not soon enough in my opinion. These kids being bused to our school from down county need help. Some of them have parents who think of them as paychecks. If I sent home another donated warm jacket only to see the same kid come in the next day without it and tell me, "My mama needed it," I'm going to need to scream or start drinking.

"Do you like Cheerios or Raisin Bran?" I asked as I reached into my secret stash. Whenever they were on sale at the supermarket I stocked up.

"Cheerios," she said.

I poured a bowl, added milk and let her eat using my desk as a table. When she finished and licked her lips free of the white mustache, I listened to her stomach again.

"Much better," I nodded my head affirming. "I think the lion went to sleep."

Keisha looked down at her stomach and said, "It feels much better."

"I'm glad, honey. Now you go on back to class and study hard okay?"

Maybe I just don't get what it's like for her parents. I can't imagine that they wouldn't feel the same joy as I do now watching their little girl trotting off to class with a full stomach.

"I hear a lion roaring in my belly too," Toby tried from his lounging position.

If anything, Toby ate too much breakfast. "I think your lion can wait until lunch," I said as I lifted the ice pack from his head. "Looks good, you have ten more minutes left of recess, you can go now."

He gave me his best "woe is me" face.

I held my ground as he shuffled down the hall.

Chapter 36

AMANDA

Justin's mom had homemade cupcakes waiting on a plate with a note that read, "I'll be right back. Went to get milk." We sat at an old round wooden table with six seats around it and dove in. I picked one with chocolate icing. He picked the vanilla. *Perfect*, I thought to myself. *We don't have to compete for the same kind the way Sarah and I do.*

With three big bites his was gone and he was reaching for another. I took my time, licking all the frosting off the top, and then unwrapping the paper cup it was baked in. The cake part was soft and almost as good as the frosting. I kinda wished his mom would get back with the milk.

"Want some water?" Justin asked with his mouth half full.

"Yes, please." I was glad 'cause now I could have another cupcake.

While he filled two glasses, I looked around the room. His mom must like chickens and roosters. There were rooster drapes along the tops of the windows, a row of canisters lined the counter each with a different type of chicken on them, and even the napkin holder in front of me had a chicken on one side and a rooster on the other. The kitchen was burnt orange, the color of our rooster's feathers at home. I looked out the window at the flat lawn. No sign of a chicken coop. Guess she didn't like them that much. Then again, we had a much bigger yard. Maybe they just didn't have enough space for them.

Justin gulped his water down and reached for a third cupcake.

"We have chickens at home," I said, wiping my hands on a napkin. I took a sip of water. "We collect our own eggs in the morning."

Justin looked at me oddly, and then the light bulb went on. He looked around the room. "Yeah, my mom grew up on a farm."

Our mothers could be friends, I thought to myself and smiled inside.

"I better leave some for my brothers or my mom will have a fit," he said looking like he could finish the whole plate of cupcakes himself.

He stood up and I followed him. We went into the family room where he had the poster boards already stacked up against the wall and glue sticks and scissors on the coffee table. I pulled the folders out of my book bag.

He laid a poster board on the floor and I sat next to him. "So, you said we should do these in categories, right?"

"Yeah, I was thinking we could do one that shows how long the different types of plastic take to biodegrade, and then one with the animals that are eating the plastic and dying in the ocean, and then one—" my conversation was cut off by Justin's mom.

"How is your project going?" she asked cheerfully from the doorway.

"Good," Justin said. "Mom, this is Amanda."

I raised my hand up and said, "Hi."

"Nice to meet you, Amanda," she said. "I see you found the cupcakes I made you." She raised an eyebrow as she zoomed in on her son.

"Yes, they were delicious, thank you," I said feeling guilty that I ate more than one. We only left three for his brothers.

"I'll be upstairs doing laundry if you need anything," she said as she turned and walk toward the stairs.

"So, let's start with the different types of plastic," Justin continued. One by one, we glued pictures of plastic bottles with the sign "450 years to decompose in the ocean." Then a diaper, also 450 years. It felt really good just to be near him. I wondered what it would be like to sit close on the big leather couch behind us watching a movie.

"Amanda."

Justin was staring at me waiting for an answer. "What? I'm sorry, what did you say?"

"I said, 'Do you want this piece over here or more towards the side,'" he placed the fishing line picture in each position so I could choose what looked best.

"Um, more towards the side," feeling embarrassed that he could catch me daydreaming about him.

We glued a picture of a T-shirt on another board and he wrote, "Recycling five plastic bottles produces enough fiber for one T-shirt."

I glued a picture of the ocean on the other side of the

board and wrote underneath it, "Almost 90 percent of floating material in the ocean is plastic. Plastic collects in huge swirls in the ocean called gyres."

When we were done we had four boards.

"It looks great," I said as I checked out all the poster boards lined up along the floor. My mom would be here in five minutes. Maybe she would meet Justin's mom and they would start talking and I could stay longer.

"We can leave them here to dry. I'll pick them up later," Justin said.

"Do you have a bathroom I could use?" I asked.

"Sure," he walked with me towards the hall with a giant mirror in the center.

As I followed him, we passed a door halfway open. I snuck a peek inside and stopped dead in my tracks.

Justin reached the bathroom doorway before he noticed I wasn't following him. "What's wrong?"

Without asking, I pushed the door open all the way. A large wooden desk with a red leather chair behind it sat on one side. On the other a big stone fireplace with two small couches faced each other in front of it. Above the mantel, hung a giant pig's head with a pissed off look and white tusks. I couldn't breathe. My eyes walked along the walls: a deer head, a moose head, a bear's head, antlers, and a stuffed bobcat. I couldn't look anymore, I felt sick.

"What? Where are you going?" Justin called out as I ran past him towards the front door. "Amanda!" he was catching up to me just as I was about to hit the sidewalk.

I felt his arm grab mine, forcing me to stop.

"That's disgusting," I shouted at him.

"What?" he looked like I was the one who was crazy.

"All those dead animals," I caught my breath.

"That's my dad," he said.

"Do you kill animals too?"

Justin's head looked down and he let go of my arm. When he didn't answer I knew that meant yes.

"How could you let me like you when you know how much I like animals?" Tears were welling up behind my eyelids, but there was no way I was letting them out; at least not in front of Justin. I was way too pissed off for that.

"Listen," he started softly and tried to reach out for my hand.

"No, you listen!" Yikes, I was sounding like my mother. "We're through, Justin. Get it. Through!" As I turned to stomp away, I saw my mother's car coming down the road. She stopped and I jumped in and commanded her to go just as his mother came out.

Chapter 37

JILL

My heart stopped when I opened my email.

An email sat on the top of the list with the subject line, "From Samantha's mom, Maria."

A reply. Taking a deep breath and holding it, I clicked it open.

Dear Jill,

Thank you so much for your letter. I shared it with Samantha.

There have been so many times I wanted to contact you. We would like to meet with you. Would you like to come to our home? I think it might help all of us.

Sincerely,

Maria

I read the last sentence again. And again. *I think it might help all of us.* *Oh, I so hope so,* I thought.

Chapter 38

AMANDA

Finally, it was the day of the science fair. I had no choice but to present our project with Justin. I decided I would never talk to him again after we finished it. As we were setting it up, Mr. Harris stopped and our display out.

"Good job, you two. This is a very big problem for our environment," he stood and raised his hand up to his chin.

We propped the last board up and he was still standing there in deep thought.

"I have an idea. What if you put a signup sheet at your display asking for volunteers to do a plastic clean up by the river? We could do it as an after school activity for extra credit," he said.

Wow, he liked it! I turned to Justin and smiled but quickly took it back. I really needed the extra credit. It would also help the animals. But, I didn't want anything else to do with Justin after this.

Justin answered for us, "Good idea, Mr. Harris. We'll do that."

I gritted my teeth. As our teacher walked away, I jabbed Justin.

"You don't have to go," he offered.

"The project was my idea," I huffed.

* * *

"Gosh, I feel so guilty. Look at what we're doing to the animals," Alice said as she signed up for the voluntary clean up. We already had over half our class sign up.

Rachel and Kailey signed up even though they were blowing me off just to prove a point.

Harley walked up to our table. Justin copped an attitude. Harley just ignored him and read our posters. "Do you mind?" he asked me as he picked up the pen to sign up.

Great, not him was my initial reaction. But then I thought, *if he helps us save even one dolphin, it would be worth it.* "Go ahead," I said.

Chapter 39

JILL

The skies were cloudy the day we were scheduled to meet. A few degrees colder and it might actually snow. Instead steady rain was in the forecast for later tonight.

Luke offered to come with me. I debated the option in my head before deciding it might be less intimidating if I went alone. A white guy with dreadlocks flashed a smile as he passed me on the sidewalk. He left behind a trail of marijuana smell. Sarah seemed to be keeping her promise not to smoke pot. She still wasn't herself lately, though. What does one do to get a teenage girl to know that she is beautiful?

I looked at my watch again, 2:45, fifteen minutes to go and I was just a block away from their apartment building. Looking around, desperate to find something to occupy the time, I spotted a community garden on a side street. I decided to head over there.

Children played whiffle ball on a fenced in basketball court that lacked a net on the hoops. A stray dog stopped to relieve himself on a fire hydrant across the road. I felt invisible which was perfectly okay with me. The community hand painted garden sign read, "Indian Valley Community Garden." Each plot was impeccably maintained. The plants were robust and bearing fruit. Two women passed by with baby carriages rapidly conversing in Spanish. I pretended like I was engrossed in the garden, while the butterflies in my stomach would have been happy to escape and suck the nectar out of a lantana.

The plan was for Maria and I to meet together first. Samantha would be home from school at 3:30. I didn't know how to prepare for this. I came straight from school wearing my routine outfit of khakis and a white cotton button-down shirt. I skipped the jewelry knowing they lived in a lower income housing area. Maybe I actually walked by them during one of my visits to Indian Valley. We often came here to go to the movie theater. What if I actually spoke to them in passing at some point? Time to walk over there, 2:47.

With each step, my chest clenched tighter. My ribs seemed to refuse to expand. The 12-story brick apartment house loomed over me. An elderly gentleman held the door open without saying a word.

"Thank you," I said as I passed alongside of him and entered the foyer.

He dipped his head forward, and then let the door close.

Each of the brass mailboxes had a name written by hand in the window of the box. Below each one, a black button. My finger perused the options until it found Hernandez and pressed their button. Silence. *Does it work*, I wondered. 2:59. *Do I press it again? I don't want her to think I'm late.* 3:00. A jarring buzz rang out and I grabbed the handle of the next door quickly while I had the opportunity and pulled it open. A foyer with a faded wooden table held a fake flower arrangement. Across was the elevator. I pushed the up arrow.

The elevator took its time getting to me. Squeaking and clunking along the way like one of my former elderly patients shuffling down the hospital hallway with their walker. When it arrived to the first floor, it took its sweet time before it opened its doors. Empty. I looked behind me, then got in. It waited until I pressed number six. Begrudgingly, it took me up there.

The dirt brown hallway carpet was well worn down the center. The light socket above my head was missing a light bulb. I unfolded the printed email stuffed in my purse to be sure I remembered the apartment number correctly. 615. To the left.

615. I stopped and tucked my hair behind my ears. My hand trembled as I raised it to knock on the door. Knock, knock, knock. I was committed now, the moment of truth. Chains clanked and then the sound of a bolt lock sliding. I watched as the doorknob turned and the door cracked open with a woman's face peering through the slit. As our eyes met, she smiled and opened the door wider.

"Jill?" she asked.

"Yes," I said. My ribs let go and let me breathe.

"Please come in," she moved behind the door and pointed towards the living room straight ahead.

The apartment was surprisingly cheery. Big south facing windows with a plant stand filled with greenery, a small TV on a side table. A deep blue couch with plump pillows and a swivel chair with giant daisy like flowers sat facing it.

"Please, can I get you something to drink?" Her voice was soft.

Scotch, straight up, tall, I wanted to say. "Water will be fine, thank you."

"Please have a seat," she offered as she went into the galley kitchen.

I chose the single chair and put my purse down alongside it on the floor. My hands were sweating. I clasped them together. A set of pictures sat on the end table by the couch. I strained to see who was in them.

"Thank you for coming," Maria gently smiled again. The water splashed in the glass as she handed it to me. Above her right eyelid was a one inch healed scar.

I took a sip. I didn't realize how parched my mouth was. She sat, took a sip of her water and looked at me, ready for me to say something.

When I didn't know where to start, she filled the void.

"Jill, I'm so relieved that you took the initiative to contact us. All these years I wanted to tell you how sorry I am. At first, I was so angry. I blamed you. But, really, the accident was my fault," she put her glass down and reached for the box of tissues on the side table. She pulled a tissue out quickly and dotted her eyes before the tears even left the sockets of her eyes.

Her fault? I was dumbfounded.

"My sister, she kept telling me how nervous her husband was. It was their first baby. He insisted on being the one to drive her to the hospital. I should have told him no. I should have stayed with her and drove her myself. She called him at work, he rushed home, the baby was not supposed to come for another week." She dabbed her eyes again. "The police officer told me he believed Raul was trying to reach into the backseat where my sister was lying down. Maybe the contractions got really bad or the baby started coming."

I placed my water glass down and got up to sit next to her. I reached my arms around her shoulders and held her as the tears turned to sobs. I reached for a clean tissue and pulled out two, one for each of us.

"It was not your fault," I managed to squeak out after a few minutes. "It was a terrible accident. I can't tell you how often I think about what would have happened if I had not been there at that time."

We bantered back and forth, desperately trying to console each other and remove each other's guilt. When we exhausted ourselves of this futile effort, she sat back and I returned to my chair.

"You will love Samantha," her smile breaking through the darkness. "She is so much like my sister. Always positive, beautiful and smart."

"I'm really looking forward to meeting her," I said.

"She's had such a hard life, but you would never know it." Maria looked down at her tissue that she was tearing to shreds. "She's lost two fathers. Her birth father and then her adopted father."

I remained silent, listening. Maria paused to collect her thoughts.

"Juan, my ex-husband was like a real father to her. He was good to us until we couldn't have a baby of our own. I found out that I have terrible endometriosis, I can't have a child." She looked up at me as if to see if I understood.

I shook my head yes.

"We couldn't afford the infertility options." She stopped again and twisted her tissue tighter. "Then, he started beating me. I worried he would hit Samantha, so we left and came back here. It broke my heart to take the only father she knew away."

The sound of a key jiggling in the lock of the door behind me startled us both. Maria sat upright and wiped her face furiously, then stuffed the tissue in her pocket. The door swung open and the girl I saw in the newspaper article appeared. She was taller, though, with a trace of mascara highlighting her doe brown eyes. She laid her backpack by the door. With the grace of a gazelle, she walked over to me with her hand outstretched. I stood up to greet her.

"Hello, I'm Samantha," her voice said softly, warmly. She walked over and hugged Maria. Then she gave her a peck on the cheek, and sat next to her on the couch.

I was too stunned to speak. Was it just Maria and I who were tortured by the accident? Samantha seemed undaunted. Not in an, "I don't give a damn," kind of way. No, more like a peaceful acceptance kind of way. Her hands with clean, polished light pink nails lay lightly on her thighs. The flawless skin on her face covered relaxed facial muscles. Her eyes were full of life, almost as if they could sparkle. Her thick shiny hair was split over her shoulders.

"I was just telling Mrs. Cooper how smart you are," Maria said as she gave Samantha a tap on her knee.

"Jill, please call me Jill."

"Mom," Samantha countered bashfully, her cheeks turning rosy. "Really, I'm not that smart," she directed to me.

"And kind," Maria added. "Samantha is going on a mission trip to Haiti with our church during Christmas break."

"Haiti?" I said trying not to let the concern in my head come through.

"Yeah, I will be going for a week," she reached up and pushed the hair on the right side of her shoulder onto her back. "I'm going to help the orphans."

Maria looked at her, then back at me. She didn't offer anything, but I could see the pride mixed with fear in her eyes. It's a look every mother knows.

"Are you going too?" I asked slowly.

Maria took a deep breath, "No," she let the breath out. "No, my mother is in the early stages of Alzheimer's and I can't get the time off from work." She began to twist the edge of her shirt the way she had the tissues.

Haiti alone. A teenage girl. A beautiful, teenage girl. My brain was the last to find out what my mouth offered. "I want to go with you."

Chapter 40

AMANDA

Taylor Swift blasted in my ears. The door to my room cracked open and Sarah peeked in.

"Don't you knock?" I said as I ripped the earphones out, Taylor still playing away.

"I did, but you weren't answering," she said as she stood in the doorway.

I looked at my iPod and turned it down, "Oh."

"Can I borrow your colored pencils?" she asked.

Sarah was a lot nicer since she broke up with Alex though she still kind of seemed bummed out.

"Sure, they're in the top drawer of my desk," I pointed from a lying position on my bed.

As she fumbled around in my drawer looking for them she turned and asked, "What are you doing home? I thought you would be hanging out with Justin or your friends?"

"Justin's history," I said. Rachel and Kailey were still kinda pissed at me, but I didn't bother sharing that with Sarah. We were planning on going to the plastic clean up after school together. Maybe we'll get back to normal then.

"Why? Did he break up with you?" Sarah looked hopeful.

"No," I said, popping her bubble. "I ditched him."

"Why?" she looked surprised.

"Because he hunts and kills animals, that's why," I sat up on the side of the bed.

"Eww, that's pretty gross. Doesn't he know the caveman days are over?" Sarah said now holding my colored pencils.

"Miss one bus, catch another," I quoted Dad's favorite saying.

"I guess," Sarah wasn't so sure. "Thanks," she raised the pack of pencils and opened my door.

"YOU WHAT?" Dad screamed from downstairs. I leapt out of bed and joined Sarah at the top of the stairs. Dad wasn't normally a yeller, but he seemed to be doing a lot of it lately. But it was usually at my sister or me.

"Jill, don't you know how dangerous it is there? It's a third world country!"

Sarah and I looked at each other and began tiptoeing down the stairs.

"But, she shouldn't go alone, she is just a teenager." Mom wasn't yelling but her tone was firm. If we lived in the West, I could picture them standing in the kitchen with their guns drawn. "It's a chance for me to give her something, to help her. It will make me feel better."

"Look, Wonder Woman. I supported you when you wanted to be a Girl Scouts leader, when you joined the PTA and all those projects, when you decided we needed to adopt a rescue dog with eye issues that required surgery. I even said okay to going to this Triton island vacation this month. But you're starting to push me over the edge. I thought we were trying to save for the girls' college education and for the new roof."

We stopped at the dining room to listen.

"You make it sound like you are the only one working. I work too," Mom fired back.

"It's dangerous," Dad said.

Sarah looked at me her eyes wider. Dangerous. Where did Mom want to go? The kitchen went silent. We couldn't take it anymore. We were going in. It was a surprise attack.

"Mom, where do you want to go?" Sarah asked.

"Your Dad and I are having a conversation." Mom said as she stood at the counter, dad just a few feet away.

"Sounds more like a fight," I mumbled.

"She wants to go to Haiti," Dad shared with us. Clearly he was trying to get us to take his side.

"Haiti? Isn't that the place where they had that bad earthquake?" Sarah asked.

"Yes," Dad nodded. "Exactly. Another reason not to go. What if that happens again? You may not be able to get out of there, or worse."

Worse? Even I knew what worse was. We moved closer to Dad.

"Mom, why would you want to go there?" I asked.

She raked her fingers through her hair. Us against her.

"I don't expect you to understand. I have an opportunity to help Samantha, that girl, whose parents died in the accident. She is going to volunteer on a mission trip to help orphans. Isn't that amazing?"

"Kind of, but what about us?" Sarah's voice began to

crack. Dad wrapped his arm around her shoulders.

Chapter 41

JILL

Truth be told, I had doubts about the Haiti trip myself. I don't know what I was thinking when I offered to go. The look of relief on Maria's face when I made the offer, made it hard to back out once my brain registered what I said. Samantha, surprisingly, seemed fine either way.

"If you want to," was all she said and shrugged. I couldn't tell if she was naïve or gracefully bold. She had an air of self-confidence I know I didn't have at her age. In fact, I'm not sure I have it at this age. But it was more than self-confidence; it was more like being self-assured.

I wanted to ask her if she was afraid, but I didn't want to instill unnecessary fear in her. "What made you decide you want to go on this mission trip?" I asked her.

She gazed at me and said, "I feel so blessed that I have family, people who love me, a home, and friends. I go to school. When our pastor did a slide show in church showing a mission trip they did over the summer, my heart broke. The orphaned children there have so little. The least I can do is go help make their lives a little better."

Her attitude humbled me. I couldn't back out on my offer.

"We have a meeting Friday night at the church," Samantha continued. "I can introduce you to our pastor. They have people who can help get you ready."

Get me ready. Shots, I knew I would need some shots, maybe malaria pills. What else would I need to get ready?

* * *

Friday night came up fast. My whole family was against me on this Haiti idea. Luke only talked to me when it was absolutely necessary. The girls seemed to ban me altogether. It felt like Peaches was my only friend in the house. If I missed feeding her a meal, that might change too.

I began to wonder if this was worth disrupting my family for. I may have changed my mind if Luke hadn't reacted so authoritarian. It was so unlike him. The deeper I got into the argument, the harder I felt it was to get out and save face. No, I will do this and they'll just have to get over it. They don't understand. They don't know what it's like to be part of someone's life ending.

The oversized parking lot was relatively empty except for about a dozen cars parked near the large doors in the front of the building. There was no cross or stained glass Jesus windows. It looked more like a two story brick office building. I parked, reached over and grabbed my purse and got out of the car. A middle-aged man with glasses pulled into the space next to me.

"You here for the mission meeting?" he asked as he hopped out of his car.

"Yes," I said unconvincingly.

"Raymond," he held out his hand, I gave him mine. He shook it vigorously. "Raymond Tilly."

"Jill Cooper." I tried to take my hand away, but he held it and looked me over.

"Nice to meet you, Jill." He let my hand go. "I haven't seen you before."

We began to walk toward the large double doors. I explained that I was new and just here to participate in the mission trip. Raymond held the door open and let me go first. The high ceiling held a giant chandelier in the center.

I was curious and nervous and suspicious. What kind of church was this?

"May I show you around?" Raymond offered. "We have a few minutes before the meeting starts."

"Um, sure, thank you. "

He walked toward a wall of doors and opened one. I peeked my head inside to find a room filled with at least two hundred chairs, a stage and three big screens raised above the stage floor. A man fussed with wires toward the back of the room. "Hey, Raymond," he said as he bent over to plug one of the wires into the wall.

"Hi, Pete," Raymond replied. "This is where we have our weekly message. As you can tell by the basketball hoops, it also serves as a gym." He pointed to the basketball backboard raised towards the ceiling. The room was dark, windowless. "It really gets rockin' in here. We have an awesome band."

I followed Raymond's lead and backed out. "See ya later, Pete."

Pete waved back.

"There are several classrooms down this hall, our baptismal area, our kitchen and then offices for our pastors." Raymond pointed upstairs.

"What denomination is it?" I asked. I had noticed that both Maria and Samantha wore crosses around their necks, so I figured it was Christian of some sort.

"We don't subscribe to any one religion," Raymond held both his hands up and flicked two fingers on both sides like a quotation sign. "We're Christian based and we're here to celebrate Jesus together. I think you might find it refreshing from the traditional, judgmental churches. At least I do."

I pondered this but remained quiet. It might actually be a refreshing change. I found myself opening to the idea.

The meeting was in this room. I let him go in first. Twenty or so people of different ages, colors, and dress styles sat or stood in groups chatting. No one was wearing a white collar. I spotted Samantha, talking to two other young girls her age. She tossed me a wave, then continued talking to the girls.

"Pastor Colby," Raymond called out to a man wearing a plaid shirt and jeans. He waited until the man was standing before us. "May I introduce you to Jill Cooper?"

"Hello, Ms. Cooper, nice to meet you," his hand outstretched to mine. His tone was casual, like we were being introduced at a barbecue. I cringed as he grabbed it knowing it was practically dripping in sweat now.

"Jill, please. Nice to meet you," my voice was quivering.

"Jill here wants to join our mission trip," Raymond told him.

Pastor Colby took his hand away and held it to his chin and thought for a second. "Are you the woman that Maria Hernandez told me about recently?"

I nodded my head.

He looked more unconvinced of this adventure than me. "Well, welcome. We'll talk more after the meeting if that is okay with you. We're about to get started."

Raymond offered the seat he stood next to. I took it before I passed out. The group gathered in a circle as Pastor Colby remained standing. He clapped his hands together, "Okay everyone, welcome." He started off with a short prayer. We bowed our heads and mumbled "Amen."

The meeting covered the preparations needed to go on the trip; a review of medical forms, vaccinations, what to bring, what not to bring, passports, and visas. I gulped hard as he talked about our security, armed with guns. Then, each member announced how far along they were in their fundraising efforts for the trip.

"Eleven hundred dollars," Raymond said.

"Five hundred."

"Seven hundred and fifty. But my grandmother told me she put a check for a hundred dollars in the mail."

The target number for each person was two thousand dollars.

Samantha lagged behind everyone. "Two hundred and twenty dollars."

Two thousand dollars! Luke was going to want a divorce. I squirmed in my chair. A woman much too young to have gray hair entered the room. She was introduced as Maggie, a mission trip volunteer from the summer. She recounted her trip and everyone in the room was riveted to her story. I looked from face to face and they all seemed genuinely excited. Pastor Colby caught my eye. I turned quickly back to Maggie.

"Would you like to go out for a cup of coffee, Jill?" Raymond asked as the group began to disperse. He reached out and held my forearm. It was then I realized that I forgot to put my wedding ring on after washing my hands when I got home. I didn't sign up for this.

"That's kind of you, but my husband and kids are waiting up for me," I said.

He removed his hand and walked away.

Samantha stopped on her way out and gushed, "Doesn't it sound exciting?"

"Yes," I lied. Yes, it would be very exciting and very worthwhile if I didn't have a family who were adamantly against it. Maybe if I was a fearless teen or a person of unshakable faith that felt this was a true calling. "Very!" I added.

"I'm sorry to rush out, but my friend's mom is giving me a ride home," she looked up at one of the girls that she was chatting with before. She was getting antsy.

"Go," I said. "I don't want to keep you."

I reached down and picked up my bag. Pastor Colby saw me and held a finger up while he finished talking to a couple. I put my bag down on the chair and looked around aimlessly.

"Can you sit for a minute?" Pastor Colby asked as the room cleared.

"Sure," I said and sat obediently, my hands placed on

my lap, my lower legs crossed.

His eyes softened, he sat back in his chair. "May I ask what is motivating you to go on this mission trip?"

I reached up and began tugging on my earring. I wrapped my foot around the leg of the chair. I looked up at the ceiling, down at the floor, towards the stack of Bibles sitting on a table in the corner of the room. I wasn't sure how much he knew already. He mentioned that he had already talked to Maria about me. I decided to give him a chance, to tell him the story. He was a pastor for God's sake. No pun intended.

I told the story starting from my doing a double shift at the hospital, to the accident, then the years of guilt and despair and wondering, then how I volunteered to go on this trip and Maria's reaction. Then onto my hope that this trip and helping Samantha might finally give me some feeling that I offered her comfort for the loss I was part of. A machine gun couldn't have spit out my words any faster. Pastor Colby sat still and listened without interruption.

He reached up and rubbed his chin. Then he leaned forward and clasped his hands together. "Jill, to be honest, I get the feeling that you are not sure about going."

His tone was kind, not accusing. He looked me directly in the eyes and sat silent waiting for my response.

I felt flustered. It felt like his eyes could look straight through me. The heat kicked on and the sound of warm air flew in above our heads.

"It's not that I don't want to go," I started. "It's just that I have responsibilities, kids, a husband, we're trying to save for college, and it's over their Christmas break. I don't have anyone to watch them." I looked into his eyes. He wasn't buying any of it. "I'm scared. I'm scared to go."

Pastor Colby smiled. "You're not alone. It's not a vacation. There are difficult things going on there in Haiti."

But I'm a nurse, I wanted to say. I can handle anything. But I kept my mouth shut and listened.

"May I make a suggestion?" he said with confidence.

I nodded, yes.

"There is another way you could help Samantha," he began. "As you heard, she is lagging behind in raising money to fund her share of the cost to go on the trip. What if you helped her raise money, rather than go?" He held his hand; palm up, like it was an offer.

The stress of the day was beginning to make my head spin. I couldn't think straight anymore. Where would I get eighteen hundred dollars in just a few weeks?

"I've already told Maria I would go. I think she would be really disappointed if I backed out now," I retorted.

"When Maria told me about your offer, she did say she was relieved someone would go with Samantha to watch out for her. But I reassured her that everyone on our mission trip would be watching out for Samantha. I can't guarantee anyone's safety, anymore than I can guarantee that we will get home safely tonight. You of all people understand that. But, we've been on this trip several times now. We've never had a problem."

I wasn't sure if I felt relieved of my duty or put out because I wasn't needed. I gave his words some thought. Again, he waited patiently for my reply. "I guess it's just that Samantha is so much stronger that I thought she would be. My God, she lost both her parents coming into this world, then her adopted father. Now she is going to help orphans when she is an orphan herself. I don't understand how she does it. I expected her to be a mess, when I decided to find her." I may as well have pushed an elephant off my lap, letting this truth free.

Pastor Colby grinned, "I know what you mean, I get it. When the Hernandezes first moved back here and joined our parish I was very concerned about Samantha. It took a while for her to warm up to me. I'm sure it wasn't easy for her to make herself vulnerable to a father figure again. But she did and we had a lot of discussions early on." He paused reflectively. "Then one day, she came in, her eyes alive and basking in joy. When I commented on how well she looked, do you know what she said?" He paused and composed himself, his eyes clouding.

I shook my head no and waited on the edge of my seat.

"She said, 'God whispered to my heart! Do you know what he told me?'" he stopped looked up and then back at me. "Now mind you, I deal with this every day and I never stop being amazed by God's grace. Samantha said, 'God told me that I have an Almighty Father who watches out for me and he will never leave me.'"

I sat in awe. Awe of her faith, her grace, and this pastor's commitment. A feeling of lack, wanting, almost jealousy rose up inside of me. What would it feel like to know that level of connection with God?

"I can assure you," Pastor Colby continued. "Samantha is in good hands."

Chapter 42

AMANDA

Without the leaves I could see more of the basalt rock that lined the river and it looked like it was almost touching the sky from down here. It lined the whole west side of the river for miles. The columns were made back in the Triassic period, something to do with molten magma and sandstone. The water running alongside the river was choppy today.

"What did your mother say about you breaking up with Justin?" Kailey asked as she leaned over and picked up another Trugoy cup. Yogurt spelled backward.

I was really glad that Kailey and Rachel were talking to me again. I was starting to get worried. "She said she wished she was as self-assured when she was my age."

"What does self-assured mean?" Rachel called from behind a bush along the graveled trail.

"I'm not exactly sure. I think it is kind of like self-confident." I turned quick and caught a glimpse of Justin at the end of our group. Almost everyone in our science class signed up for the clean-up. He was talking to Harley. I turned my head back fast before they caught me looking.

"There sure are a lot of cups from Trugoys," Rachel held up a clear plastic cup with a plastic cover and straw still in it.

Kailey and I opened our pillowcases and looked into them.

"Yeah, I noticed that too," I said.

"Almost half my bag is Trugoy cups and bowls," Kailey added.

"Trugoys might have the best frozen yogurt, but this is crazy," Rachel joined us back on the path, wiped the hair out of her face with her forearm and let her bulging pillow case rest on the ground.

"Maybe Mr. Harris can help us talk to the store about it," Kailey suggested.

"Maybe," I nodded and then continued on closer to the water's edge. A bottle top and six-pack holder bobbed in between the rocks. I bent down and pulled them out, shook them off and added them to my loot.

We were getting closer to the spot where the dolphin died. I looked out at the water flowing in tiny waves toward New York City. How many dolphins have died out there in the ocean that we don't even know about from all this garbage?

I willed myself not to cry, remembering my mother's advice. "One of the best ways to honor someone you have lost is to do something positive in their memory."

All along the river's edge my classmates held pillowcases bulging and nearly overflowing with plastic and other garbage we found. I never really knew how cool they could be.

"Can we just stop for a moment?" Mr. Harris waved us towards him.

We gathered around him.

"Who can tell me what type of rock this is?" He turned around and pointed at the cliffs that looked like a row of tree trunks.

"Basalt!"

Alice. I didn't even have to turn and see who said it. My eyes followed the crevices in the rock. It was as if someone sliced a cake then picked at the sides with a fork.

"And who can tell me is this sea water or fresh water," Mr. Harris held his hand above his eyes with one hand and pointed toward the river with the other.

We turned.

"It's brackish," David answered like he was on *Jeopardy!* or something. Alice pounded her first against her thigh. Across the river, buildings from towns that I can't remember the names of poked out on the other side.

"Good, oh, we'll go just a little bit more. It looks like most of your bags are almost full." He took a gander at the bags we let sit at our feet. He began to turn to go further along the trail but Rachel stopped him.

"Um, Mr. Harris," she said.

He stopped and looked at her.

Rachel pointed ahead. "That's where the dolphin died, up there just past that big tree." Her voice sounded shaky. We all stopped and looked ahead. No one said a word, which never happened in our class. The river lapped over and over. A cloud blocked the sun. Something, a squirrel or a bird maybe, kicked up leaves next to us in the brush.

Kailey wiped her eyes. I swallowed hard.

"Well," Mr. Harris finally broke the silence. "Today you might be saving a dolphin or a bird or a turtle. You just never know."

Chapter 43

JILL

The light to the den seeped through the curtains as I pulled in the driveway. The rest of the house was dark except for the porch light by the back door. I turned the ignition off and leaned my head back on the headrest.

Pastor Colby gave me an out, a solution to my internal dilemma. But would Maria be disappointed? I couldn't bear seeing her or Samantha hurt again by me. And what about my family? Was I really going to let my stubborn, independent pride and determination hurt my marriage? Make my girls worry about my safety?

I got out of the car, clicked the door closed gently and looked up at the starless sky. *I know you're there*, I said to my mother silently. Oh how I wish I could just go and sit at the kitchen table in our old house and talk this over with her. *Tell me what to do. At least give me a hint.* Several minutes passed. Nothing. Goosebumps rose on my arms. I could see my breath. Finally I gave up and went inside.

The downstairs was dark except for the glow of the light coming from the den. I could barely make out the two bowls that sat in the sink one on top of the other. I lay my purse on the counter and tiptoed toward the den.

I unwrapped the scarf from my neck and laid it on table in the hall. The house was dead silent. The den was empty. Luke didn't wait up. Half disappointed and half relieved, I plopped down on the couch and hugged a throw pillow. I didn't realize it was that late at 10:12. Peaches waddled in, hoisted herself up onto the couch and planted her big chin on my thigh with a thud. Her warmth soaked into me. *At least someone in this house loves me*, I thought. My fingers raked through her soft fur and massaged her floppy ears.

A gust of wind howled outside. My eyes scanned the room, and then rested on the wooden rocking chair across from me. In it sat the doll my mother made. Her yellow braids dangled in front of her shoulders, her permanent grin cheery as usual. But tonight, her eyes, her button eyes were different, deeper. My eyes stared into hers and for a few precious moments time was lost. Then it hit me, an ever so gentle whisper to my heart.

I jumped off the couch, leaving Peaches with a startled and annoyed look on her face. I rushed over and snatched the doll up. I held it up in the air, and looked her in the face, "You're a genius!" I whispered loudly as the two of us twirled like we were star dancers.

My eyes opened a good half hour before my alarm clock was due to jolt me out of my normal dead sleep. Luke snored gently beside me, one arm draped over his head, the other on top of the comforter. Slowly, I rolled out of bed, slid my feet into my slippers and quietly picked up my bathrobe and slid my arms into it as I left the room. I was just as excited this morning as I was when I went to bed. *A good sign*, I thought, one that I had hoped for when I decided to sleep on my decision.

I tiptoed into the kitchen, made the coffee, and then pulled out all the fixin's to make a scrumptious pancake breakfast for my family. As I hummed "Good Morning, Sunshine" and whisked the batter, the sun began to rise. The floorboards creaked above my head. I flicked a blob of butter onto the cast iron frying pan and waited for it to sizzle.

One by one my family entered the kitchen as I piled the warm flapjacks onto a plate and placed it on the center of the table next to the heated authentic maple syrup. The girls and Luke looked at each other suspiciously, then at me. I said nothing. They sat and eyed the breakfast great temptation. Luke broke the ice.

"You're awfully cheery this morning." He took the top four pancakes with a fork and his fingers. The girls battled for the next layer. They passed the syrup to each other after their own plate was drenched with the sweet smelling tree sap.

"Yes, I am." I shoveled the last of the pancakes off the griddle and laid them on top of the dwindling pile. I joined them at the table with my coffee cup half full. They watched me with their heads tilted up, chewing and scooping up the next fork full of food. My heart filled with joy watching them enjoy the meal I just prepared for them. At the same time, I chuckled to myself inside as they tried to figure out what gives.

"I'm not going to go to Haiti," I announced.

The news sent their forks dropping to the table.

"You're not?" Sarah asked half not believing what I just said.

"No," I said firmly. "I'm going to help Samantha raise the money to go on the mission trip."

My youngest looked from me to Sarah to her father.

"Thank God," Luke got up, came to me and leaned over to hug me. In his I-don't-know-if-I-want-to-hear the answer voice, he asked. "How much does she need to go?"

"One thousand eight hundred dollars." To my surprise, he didn't sound gruff; his eyebrows wrinkled just a bit though.

"How are you going to raise the money?" Sarah asked as she resumed eating.

"You know that doll my mother made? The one that is sitting on the rocking chair in the den?" I said.

Everyone nodded yes.

"Well," I continued. "I'm going to make dolls like that and sell them. Custom dolls so people can have whatever eye color, hair and dresses on them that they want. The profits will all go to help fund Samantha's trip. Since Christmas is coming up, I thought I might be able to sell a few." I took a sip of coffee and let the idea settle in as the warmth trickled down the back of my throat.

Chapter 44

BANE

HAWAII 1998

Only his mother could get them to gather so close. Today was her fiftieth birthday. The only thing she asked for was a party with her family. Bane's toddler nieces and nephews sat close to the two-tiered white cake decorated with plumeria flowers. Bane's two older sisters held infant babies in their arms. His brother-in-laws chatted behind them.

Bane sat at the table with the kids and gently reminded them not to touch the cake. He could feel his father's glaring eyes all the way from across the table. *Couldn't he just let it go for today?* Bane wondered to himself.

Nanea bounced around from one guest to the other thanking them for coming to her party. She stood on her tippy toes to reach up and kiss each one while bear hugging the kids. Her dark black eyes twinkled. She was starting to gray, Bane noticed. When she reached Bane, she stood back and held her hands out. "Having you here makes it extra special." As she wrapped her arms around her only son,

Bane could hear his father's teeth grit.

How could such a sweet woman marry such an ogre, he wondered. Did growing up the son of a Pearl Harbor survivor harden him? Was he always so opinionated and stubborn? He got a steal marrying her. Maybe back then, dressed in a Navy uniform, with a good paying job, he seemed a catch too.

"Let's blow out the candles together," Nanea announced to the kids as each of the five candles representing ten years was lit. Their eyes opened wide with excitement.

"Wait, we have to sing happy birthday first," Bane's oldest sister reached her hand out.

With that, they all bellowed the celebratory words. All of them, except his father.

Chapter 45

JILL

Triton

We boarded the plane just as the sun's rays lightened the sky.

"I want the window seat," Amanda said as she walked down the aisle with her backpack on, following Luke.

"I want the window seat," Sarah answered behind me.

"There are two window seats, you can each have one," I looked down at the boarding passes, Aisle 18, just two more down. "That's our aisle," I pointed and Luke stopped. "Three seats on each side, perfect. Amanda, you sit in that window seat, Dad and I will sit with you. Sarah, you sit in that one, and Grandpa and Lois will sit next to you." The girls did as they were told. The men each took the aisle seats so they could stretch out their long legs. My father tucked his briefcase under the seat in front of him.

"You're not going to work the whole time, are you?" I overheard Lois say to my father as I leaned over to help Sarah get buckled in. "Luke, will you just make sure that Amanda has her seat belt on?" He leaned over the other row of seats.

"Really, Mom?" Amanda said. "I'm not a baby. I can buckle myself."

Just a few intermittent empty seats remained. It was the same type of traveler that I remembered from my trip to Triton years ago. Divers, vacationers, women going on a girls' getaway and honeymooners cooing at each other. "Remember when we were like that?" I poked at Luke.

"Pre-kids," was all he had to say.

"How long will we be in the air?" Sarah asked.

"Just a few hours." Neither of the girls showed any fear of flying despite this being only their second flight in their lifetime. The first was a trip to Disney World when they were younger. Amanda strained to look out over the tarmac.

"I never realized how big these planes are," she proclaimed. I peeked over at Sarah who was doing the same and gabbing with Lois.

"Good morning, ladies and gentlemen. Welcome to Flight 1132 direct to Triton Island. We will be taking off shortly. Please make sure that your seatbelts are securely fastened. The flight attendants will be passing through the cabin in case anyone needs help."

The flight attendants went through the routine emergency preflight directions. Amanda looked at me with worry, but I patted her hand. "It's just a precaution." She relaxed her shoulders and turned to look at the window.

The roaring of the engines rumbled through my body. As the plane lifted into the sky, I felt like we were leaving all our stresses behind. I had no doubt many of them would be waiting for us in the terminal when we landed. For now,

I imagined them watching us leave as we flew far, far away.

* * *

The flight was smooth. The bagel with cream cheese and fruit cup they served tied us over. My father broke out his briefcase and reviewed all kinds of documents. Lois and Sarah played several rounds of hangman. Luke slept most of the flight while I leafed through the latest issue of *O, The Oprah Magazine* that I picked up in the airport before we boarded. Amanda never stopped looking out the window except for when she would turn to me to report the latest marvel.

"Look at the clouds," she exclaimed. "If we got out of the plane, could we walk on them?"

She was my inquisitive one, always wondering and questioning.

The pilot announced that we were going to begin our descent; I brushed Amanda's shoulders to catch a glimpse of the approaching islands and the kaleidoscope of colors surrounding them.

"Mom, the water is so many bright colors!"

I felt the same sense of awe as my daughter when I saw the sun's radiance and crystal clear water. What more was to come? Relaxing days lying on the chaise lounges by the sea, fresh conch and fruit, snorkeling among the reefs, I could hardly contain my excitement. I would get to experience it all again and this time share it with my family. Deep inside, a thought nudged again, threatening my delight, *what if we run into Bane?*

Chapter 46

AMANDA

I stood next to Sarah as we waited for our luggage to be thrown onto the long platform with the others. Grandpa paced and looked at his watch repeatedly. Lois and Mom chatted while my dad tried to sneak a peek through the flap door that the luggage was coming through.

"Did you see how blue the ocean is here?" I tried to get Sarah excited.

"Yeah, it was pretty," she replied in her I-don't-really-care tone as she twirled her finger in her ponytail.

Great, I thought to myself. *I hope she shakes off her pissy mood. She's the only one I have to do things with here.*

"Ours is coming," my dad announced like we should position ourselves for a football play.

One by one we claimed our luggage and lugged it out to the curb. The tropical heat mugged us like moist towels. We all shrieked and covered our squinting eyes like vampires when we got outside. We couldn't find our sunglasses fast enough. Except, of course, for my grandfather who casually pulled his out of his jacket pocket and put them on. *Gosh, why didn't he warn us,* I wondered.

I followed my parents closely after noticing a small group of men hanging out on a nearby bench eyeing my sister and me. They gave me the creeps.

"That's it, over there," my mother pointed to a yellow van. Several people were already sitting inside.

"You going to Sea and Sand?" a dark black woman with gray hair asked us.

"Yes, maybe we'll wait for the next bus," my dad answered as he restrained Mom with his arm. "Looks like you're almost full."

"Go on, get in, plenty of room," she shoved us toward the van and we obeyed. We left our luggage for my dad to load in the very back and squeezed into the last two rows of seats.

After my dad wedged himself into the last spot next to Grandpa, he pulled the door shut after two tries. The old woman hurled herself into the driver's seat. Sarah and I looked at each other, trying not to let her see us as we wondered if she was capable of driving this big van.

A thin man wearing the same uniform as our driver shouted to her, "You gonna need to come back, there more guests here."

"I'll be back," she shouted out the window as she rested one arm on the open window and pulled away from the curb.

Grandpa reached into his chest pocket, retrieved a handkerchief and wiped his forehead. Dad, on the other hand, just used the back of his hand to wipe his. The wind winding through the bus was as productive at cooling us down as a soaked sponge trying to wipe up spilled milk.

We rode quietly, no one wanting to add anymore heat to the situation. Dust kicked off the back of the van while our driver dodged potholes. It reminded me of how Sarah avoids the moguls on the black diamond trails.

"Look, a donkey." I pointed out the window at a mule grazing on the edge of the road.

"You'll see plenty of those here on the island," our driver shouted back at us as she looked in the review mirror. "Horses, chickens, maybe even some cows too." Then she jerked the van and we all were tossed to the right, "Sorry about that, that was a big one."

"Christ, what is this, Gilligan's Island?" Grandpa muttered.

Lois ignored him and pointed out more donkeys grazing on the few mounds of grass in an open field on the other side of the road.

What we saw of the island so far was unimpressive. It looked the way Rachel described Arizona after a visit there, minus the cactus. When we entered the resort it all changed. Bushes with leaves all different colors; red blending with orange and yellow, pink with purple veins all loaded with bright, cheery flowers the size of our hands lined the driveway.

When we reached the lobby the van doors flew open before the driver shut off the ignition. One by one everyone hopped out. Sarah shot me a grossed out look as I peeled my sweaty arm away from hers, like I did it on purpose.

A group of happy people dressed in blue and white flowered shirts and khaki shorts gathered around us, excited to take our bags. I let mine go after seeing my parents give theirs away.

"We're all together," my mother told one guy as she pointed at me, Sarah and Dad. The man nodded and placed all our bags on one rolling rack.

We waited on the check-in line, the breeze now cooling us down. The lobby had no doors. Big green plants that almost touched the ceiling waved with the wind. Long cushy couches were grouped together. *Maybe we could play cards there*, I thought.

"Next, please," a man stepped behind the counter and waved us toward him. We marched single file to the desk.

"We're the Coopers," Dad said as he reached into his pocket for his wallet.

As the man searched in his computer for our name, Mom yelled, "Darly! You're still here."

Clearly surprised that someone knew his name, the man popped his head up and looked at Mom. He scrunched his eyes in silence.

"Jill. Jill Cooper, now. I was Jill Bradley when I was here, several years ago. I'm sorry. You probably don't remember me. You were a bellhop back then. You really helped me out, I was here alone."

Darly's eyes opened wide and his eyebrow rose, "Miss Jill, of course I remember you!" He reached both of his hands across the desk and Mom put hers in his.

"Wow, you're the assistant manager now." Mom's eyes looked his nametag.

"Yes, have been for five years now," he lifted his chin in the air and looked at each of us, then back to Mom. "So happy to have you come back."

Mom introduced us and pointed out Grandpa and Lois standing in the next line. Darly's face changed when Mom mentioned that we were here because Grandpa was thinking of investing down here. I think Mom noticed it too because her smile faded when she saw his reaction.

A line was forming behind us so Darly stopped talking and got us checked in. "You have adjoining rooms. There are four keys in here and a bracelet for each of you. As you know, you'll need to wear the bracelet at all times in order to get in the dining areas and use the sports equipment. We have a lot of new activities." He opened a folder and pointed out a brochure with a picture of a paddle boarder on it.

"Look, they have paddle boarding," I nudged Sarah who only shrugged her shoulders.

"Anything you need, you know you only have to ask," Darly finished.

Mom looked back at the growing line behind us. "Thank you, Darly."

Dad reached over the desk and shook his hand. We gathered our things and followed the bellhop to our rooms.

* * *

Our rooms were a few doors down from Grandpa and Lois. The door that separated Sarah's and mine from our parents was locked. The keys we had been given didn't work on this one.

"Tell you what." Mom said in her "I've got this all

figured out tone." "Why don't you all go to the main dining room for lunch? I'll meet you there after I stop at the front desk to get the key for that door."

"Good, I'm hungry." Sarah said, finally showing an interest in something.

Chapter 47

JILL

Darly was looking over the shoulder of one of the desk clerks at the computer screen. "Yes, we do have an oceanfront room available." He told the clerk to give the waiting guests that one instead of the inner courtyard. The desk clerk nodded and I noticed the dazzling bling of her engagement ring as she clapped her hands.

"Thank you, sir," the young man said with a southern drawl. "Much appreciated."

"My pleasure," Darly patted the clerk on the shoulder and headed my way when he saw me standing there in the lobby.

"I'm really so pleased you are here again," he reached out and put his hand on my shoulder.

"I'm very excited to be back. I'm so glad to see things working out for you."

"Yes, they workin' out real well, bless the Lord. I moved my mother to the island here, so now I don't have to worry about her."

"That's terrific. I bet she's thrilled to be closer to you too."

Darly nodded. "And, look at you, you have a beautiful family of your own now."

"Yes," I agreed. The smell of warm salty air led my thoughts back in time. *What happened to Trina?* I never heard any more from the nurse who helped me deliver Trina's baby during my last visit. "Do you ever hear anything about that girl, Trina? The nurse from the hospital wrote me once that she and the baby went to live with relatives on another island."

"Oh, yes, Trina is doing very well. She went to live with Reverend Taylor and his wife. They raised her proper. Trina has a good job in the immigration department in Jamaica and her daughter doing good in school. One of my kitchen staff is related to them so she keep me up to date. Good thing you was there to deliver her baby, otherwise she probably would have died."

"And Nettie?" I asked cautiously.

"Nettie went to be with the Lord," Darly reached his arm out again and patted my shoulder.

We stood quiet. I wanted to ask Darly about Bane. I wasn't longing for him, although the romantic memories felt good. I loved my husband. I guess I was just curious. I also wanted to prepare myself in case I was to see him.

I coughed even though nothing was clogging my throat. "Actually, I came down here to see if you could help me. The door that adjoins our rooms is locked. The keys we have won't open it."

Without missing a beat, Darly pointed to a young man standing by the front entrance, "Terence, I need you to go to Room 212 and unlock the adjoining door, please."

The boy, in the position Darly was in when I first met him, sprang into action.

I looked at Darly. "Thank you."

He smiled as I headed toward the dining room.

As I walked down the crushed shell pathway lined with luscious, tropical plants, I stopped to soak in the magnificent ocean ahead. *Please, Sharky, if you can hear me, will you just come and say hello, just for a minute while we are here?* I began to turn when I noticed out of the corner of my eye, a faint rainbow far off in the distance. There was hope.

I found my family surrounded by plates of food. Clearly their taste buds went into overdrive at the buffet table. Chicken kabobs with jerk sauce, pasta salad, shrimp cocktail. "Are you going to eat all that?" I asked. Clearly I didn't feed them enough at home.

They nodded yes as they continued to shovel in the food. "Where's my dad?" I asked Lois who simply had a healthy portion of snapper and mixed salad on her plate.

"He had a quick bite then went to meet with his developer friends," she patted her mouth gently with her napkin then placed it back in her lap.

I went to gather my lunch. When I returned my family were just slowly moving the food on their plates around. If I had waited a few minutes, I could have easily just eaten what they wouldn't be able to finish. "Okay, so now we have all learned a lesson here. Next time, take a little bit at a time at the buffet, you can always get up and get more." They leaned back and breathed deeply.

"So, what would you like to do this afternoon?" I asked.

Amanda was the first to answer, like she was competing

in a game show. "I want to try paddle boarding!"

I looked at Sarah who still had her frowny face on. You would think we brought her to Siberia. Is she really going to sit here and pout all weekend because she missed a football game?

"I'm not going in the water, I don't want to get my hair wet," she replied sliding the blow-dried strands through her fingers.

Luke looked at me, then took a stab at engaging her. "Sarah, we are in this beautiful place, why don't you take advantage of what it has to offer."

"I don't want to. I will sit by the pool and read."

Lois chimed in, "Sarah, honey, I brought a good book too. Would you mind if I sat and read with you?"

"That's fine," she said graciously. Thank goodness.

So with our bellies satisfied, Sarah pulled out the latest Sarah Dessen novel and headed for the pool area with Lois. Lois seemed to be taking more interest in the girls now that they were older. She never was the type to offer to babysit when they were younger. She would prepare a treat if we visited their home and she bought nice gifts for their birthdays and Christmas but that was about the extent of it. I was never sure if she didn't want to seem like she was taking over what would have been my mother's role or if she just didn't want to be burdened with the massive work of caring for young children.

"I'll meet you down at the beach, okay?" Luke said as he stood up. "I noticed they had some good cigars in the gift shop."

He acknowledged my glare but he shrugged his

shoulders, lifted his hands in the air and said, "Hey, we're on vacation," and left.

Left alone with Amanda, we each grabbed a banana for the beach and set out to find the water activities shack. "Do you think we'll see that dolphin you were telling me about?"

My heart sank a little. "I hope so. You have to keep in mind, though, that he is a wild dolphin. He isn't trained like the captive ones that you see in the commercials." Amanda nodded her head and I explained to her the etiquette that Bane had taught me years ago if we did encounter Sharky.

The water sports shack was at the far end of the resort, just where it was when I was last there although several new buildings stood behind it. We sauntered down the beach, side by side, as a tender breeze wafted our hair behind us. *Even if we didn't see Sharky, moments like this would make it all worth it*, I thought to myself.

Chapter 48

AMANDA

I couldn't get over how amazing the ocean colors were here. The first several feet along the beach were so clean it was colorless, just like bathwater. After that it started with a tint of aquamarine, then merged into the blue the color of a swimming pool. The shades of blue deepened as the water got deeper.

I held my flip flops in my hand and walked through the ripples of water rolling onto shore. The sun was so bright it felt like you couldn't hide from it.

Kayakers, kiteboarders and paddleboarders dotted the water in the distance. I could hardly wait; I had wanted to try paddle boarding for a long time. "Do you think it's hard?" I asked my mom.

She nodded ahead at an old guy heading back in to beach on one. "I think if he can do it, we can."

I was glad she seemed confident, since I was really more worried about her trying this than me.

By the time we got near the water sports shack the older man was at the desk returning his paddle. We waited patiently behind him.

"That was great fun! I saw schools of fish swimming under me, should have brought my fishing pole," he jested.

"That would take some good balancing," the tan shirtless, guy with curly chin length hair replied as he hung the paddle up on the wall with the others.

"I guess I better practice some more before I try that then." The old man turned and waved. "Thanks again, maybe I'll be back tomorrow."

"We'll be here, have a good day," the young guy said as he leaned forward onto the counter and at us. "What can I do for you?" His teeth were perfectly straight and white. When he looked at me I saw more of them and that made me feel special.

"Hi, we'd like to try paddleboarding," my mom announced.

"If it's your first time, we have a beginners' class that starts in a half hour; I'll be teaching it actually."

Mom looked at me and I shook my head yes.

"Okay, it will be the two of us and maybe my husband." Mom looked down the beach for a sign of Dad.

"No problem, I will you put you down for three. I have two already signed up." He came out from the shack holding two life preservers. "Try these on and see how they fit." We did and with only minor adjustments they fit just fine. "Leave these on the desk here. In a half hour meet me by those racks." He pointed at a small cluster of racks holding only one kayak.

"Great, thank you," Mom replied and we set out for a couple of lounge chairs just a short distance away. We left our stuff on the chairs, stripped off our clothes and painted her 100 proof sunscreen lotion on. "You're going to want to be extra careful in this sun."

Dad started to appear far off with a cloud of smoke trailing above him.

"Don't say anything," Mom interrupted me before I could get my concern out. "He knows it's not good for him, but it's his choice to make."

I opened my mouth to say, "But ..." and she shut me down.

"He doesn't do it that often," she looked at me and I knew by her tone that if he did, she would get to him first.

We waded into the water just up to our ankles so the sunscreen we put on could sink into our skin. It was so warm. Sarah didn't know what she was missing. We stood quietly. I gazed down at my toes and watched tiny fish swim by while Mom seemed to let the stress ooze out of her body and wash away with the tide. What a relief, she's been so uptight lately.

I looked up and scanned across the smooth water that gently rolled towards us. *How would we know if that dolphin is here*, I wondered. "Do you think we'll see Sharky today?"

Mom looked out into the horizon. "I hope so," not sounding as enthusiastic as she was when she first told me about the dolphin. I shrugged it off. Maybe she was just tired.

Dad came up trying to swipe the cigar smoke away from us. "I better stand downwind."

"We're all set to take lessons in a few minutes, we saved you a spot," Mom told him.

"Great!"

He was more excited than I thought he would be. We sent him off to get fitted for his lifevest as the previous session of paddle boarders began to row in.

Learning to paddle turned out to be easier than I thought it would be. Laird, our instructor, adjusted the length of our paddles for each of us so we would get the most bang for our rowing. He taught us the basics; how to paddle forward, backward and turn. As we practiced balancing in the shallow water he had each of us get down on our knees and back up a few times. "You will always want to row out and in on your knees so you don't hit something and go flying off."

When everyone felt confident, Laird sent us out one by one while he followed behind. Dad led the way, his paper white skin screaming tourist. There was very little wind, which apparently was a good thing for us, not so good for the kite boarders. Mom and I paddled side by side.

"I really hope I get to see Sharky," I shared with Laird as he caught up to us.

"Haven't seen him around for a while now." Then he paddled faster to the woman ahead of us who was veering off to the right too much.

My good mood deflated like a tire. I paddled one last time then let the board drift.

"He's wild, honey. We'll just have to wait and see."

I started paddling again, but my enthusiasm was gone.

"Let's stay kind of close together," Laird looked back at us and waved us closer. Dad was several yards ahead. Since when did he become Mr. Sports Guy?

With a few hard strokes we caught up to the group. Laird stopped us, had us kneel down as he demonstrated falling off and how to get back on. "Feel free to jump off now that we are out here. It's about 12 feet deep. Since it's relatively calm, we will head almost to the reef area." Laird pointed way out to where the ocean was a darker shade of blue. "We do have a rescue boat if anyone gets into trouble. If you get too tired, though, let me know. Otherwise, enjoy the ride." With that he set out for the wild blue yonder.

Eventually we caught up to Dad as his stamina wore off. The three of us sat down and straddled our boards, letting our legs dangle in the ocean. "This is pretty awesome," he said as he looked down around him.

I remained quiet and let the bob of the gentle waves rock me. I liked this feeling, even when I was kayaking. I imagined it was like being rocked in a rocking chair in my mother's lap. The motion put me into a trance.

"Hey, Amanda!" Laird yelled from afar. "Look, over there, it's Sharky!" He pointed due west, the glare of the sun bouncing off of the ocean making it difficult to see.

I immediately stood up. I didn't see anything except burning light and a sailfish sun boat tacking back and forth.

"Is that him?" Dad pointed. "I saw a dark thing pop out of the water. He's way over there."

I paddled faster towards where Dad was pointing. My parents tried to keep up, but I didn't wait. I still didn't see anything so it was hard to know where to go. My mom's voice was calling behind me, pretty far away, "Amanda, wait for us!"

I let the paddleboard glide forward and watched like a pirate in the crow's nest of the ship. Nothing. I scanned back and forth, then back and forth again. Nothing.

"Swooosh."

I knew that sound immediately. Sharky was coming at me from my left side.

"Swooosh." He took a breath then dove out of sight. In a flash he was circling below my board, a gray indistinguishable mass. As quick as he came, he left. I watched him surface for air yards away heading towards the reef.

"Wow, he came right near you," Dad cheered as he paddled long deep strokes. Mom struggled to keep up behind him.

I sat down on the board again. "Yeah, that was pretty cool."

He sat down too and pulled water up to wash away the sweat on his face. Wiping the salt out of his eyes he said, "You look disappointed."

"He swam away." I looked out to see if he was still by the reef but there was no sign of him. "I wanted to look at him in the eye."

Chapter 49

JILL

"Did you have fun?" Lois asked as she sipped on a pina colada while lounging in a cushioned chaise lounge with a book spread open in her lap. Her short silver gray hair barely showed under the large brimmed straw hat. For an oversized woman she maintained herself well. The slightly sheer cover up exposed the modest black bathing suit she wore underneath.

"Yes, it was great," I said as Luke stared at Sarah who was now picking up a pina colada from the cocktail table between them.

"It's virgin." She smirked.

"Amanda saw a wild dolphin, we think it was Sharky." I turned and looked at Amanda who was pulling up an armchair.

"That's wonderful," Lois beamed. Her bright blue eyes complemented the surroundings.

"Yeah, but it only swam underneath my board and then it left," she leaned forward in her chair.

"Is that all we are going to do on this trip is talk about dolphins?" Sarah complained.

If I hadn't birthed them both myself, I would wonder if they were really sisters sometimes. They were so different. And yet when they connected, they connected on a deep level. Lately they were more like feral cats eyeing and hissing at each other.

Before I could answer, my father paraded over to us, an unusual jubilant spring in his step. Lois noticed it too, "Boy, you look happy, I guess your meeting went well."

"It did. We've all been invited on Mr. Whittier's yacht for dinner tonight," he announced.

Luke and I chuckled as we overheard the girls talking in the next room while we gussied ourselves up.

"What exactly do you do on a yacht?" Amanda asked.

"You mingle and talk, eat fancy food, but not too much, you don't want to look like a pig," Sarah told her as if she went yachting on a regular basis. In truth, she was the only one in our family with any yacht going experience. She has a friend back home, Lindsey, whose father is very wealthy, something to do with hedge funds. Luke and her dad have talked several times at the high school footballs games. They too wanted to raise their children in a quiet suburban atmosphere, but spent half their time in their Manhattan penthouse. Luke found him to be very down to earth. I made very little connection with her mother, however, despite my fervent attempts to be friendly. Discussing the latest fine places to dine or shop was not engaging to me.

Lindsey's family was always very kind and generous to Sarah, though. Last summer they invited her to spend two weeks in the Hamptons. My daughter came back with a newly acquired taste for the finer things, which my husband used to explain how she would need to study extra hard to support that.

"Maybe we should get some tips from Leona," Luke whispered as he tightened his tie. "Is this tie okay? It's the only one I brought. Good thing you told me to pack one just in case."

It was a little loud with bright yellow, orange and neon green diamonds. I think he was thinking tropical when he packed. I didn't dare laugh or reply with a comment that would make him feel self-conscious. "It's perfect."

He stood back and eyed himself in the mirror.

I wasn't sure I brought something appropriate to wear on a yacht either. I decided on the simple white linen dress and added the navy shawl for a dash of nautical. I wondered if the Whittiers would notice that my pearl earrings and matching necklace that I bought at Marshalls were fake. I for one, couldn't tell the difference. And I'm sure they weren't going to try and chew on them to see if they were gritty, at least that is what I heard is the way that you can tell if they are real.

"Are you girls ready?" I called out.

"I am," Amanda answered as she came into our room and then sat on the edge of the bed waiting.

Amanda dressed the best she could with what she packed too. The moisture from the sea made her curly hair form ringlets that fell loosely just below her shoulders. She wore the light pink dress we picked out from the Gap and white sandals.

"You look lovely," I told her.

"Amanda, did you take my silver bracelet?" Sarah asked as she strode into our room wearing her sequin black formfitting dress and black leather short pumps that we got for her to go to last year's Christmas Ball at school. Her hair was slicked back and wrapped in a twist with pins of some sort that had jewels on the tips. Her baby fresh skin was brushed ever so slightly with blush, her eyes bold with the mascara we let her start wearing and eye shadow that I had no idea she had.

I felt Luke turn to say something and shot him the "don't say a word" look. Poor Luke. He grew up with brothers. Converting to a home full of estrogen was a constant struggle.

"You look lovely, too." Sarah smiled at my outfit.

"Where did you get the eye shadow?" I said, throwing my hands on my hips.

"Lois let me borrow it."

I nodded. Lois and I would need to have a little chat. "Let's go. I told Grandad that we would meet him and Lois in the lobby."

* * *

We pulled into the harbor that was just a short ride from the resort. It was lined with mostly fishing boats, a couple of rescue boats, then alternating rows of bow riders, cabin cruisers and sailboats. At the very end of the furthest dock, taking nearly half the dock space was an enormous dark blue and gleaming white yacht.

"We're going on that?" Amanda asked voicing my thoughts.

"Yup," my father said as he handed cash to the driver that Darly had arranged for us.

I smoothed my skirt and Luke tightened his tie. Lois looked at me and raised her eyebrows. Sarah reached out for Luke's hand to hold her steady so her heels wouldn't fall in between the slots of the dock as we sauntered down toward our destination, trying to pull off the impression that we had done this before. I felt more like we were on an episode of *The Beverly Hillbillies*.

A plank reached down from the boat to the dock and a clean-cut man in his twenties dressed in a Captain Stubing's white uniform greeted us. "Welcome, may I assist you onboard?" Dad took Lois's arm and the two of them went first, followed by Luke and our rock star daughter, while Amanda and I each held onto the arm of the fit young man.

Another gentleman, slightly older, offered us champagne as we stood in awe of the luxury around us. The brass and teak trimmings were finely polished, the cushions along the benched edges were supple white leather, and this was just the beginning. "We have sparkling cider for the ladies," he pointed at two glasses on the outer rim of his tray. Amanda and Sarah each took one, Amanda trying to play princess, Sarah already crowned.

"Mr. Whittier and Mrs. Whittier will join you shortly," he said and left us to ourselves.

"This is nicer than our house," I whispered to Luke.

"You think?" he replied.

"Greetings, welcome aboard the *Champagne Taste*," said a

tall man wearing pristine white gabardine trousers and a navy blue blazer with nautical rope emblems on the buttons. A navy colored scarf instead of a tie twisted around his neck, complete with polished penny loafers, with an actual penny in the slot on the top. His thick salt and pepper hair was slicked back to expose his deeply tanned face. The ocean breeze delivered his seducing scent to my nostrils. I couldn't identify it.

Behind him followed a tall, voluptuous woman, wearing a floral patterned maxi dress that barely contained her breasts. Luke wrapped his arm around me. My father stood in a bolt upright position, his eyes embarrassingly staring right at her chest. Lois shot him a glare and he returned his focus to our host.

"Gable, I would like you to meet my family," Dad introduced us one by one and each of us shook Mr. Whittier's hand. The beautiful woman now stood next to him and just bowed her head at us. Latina I guessed.

"I'm so glad you could join us. This is Isabel," he whisked his two arms toward her like he was featuring a prize on *The Price is Right*. She nodded at us again and gave a closed lip smile. We clumsily waved or bowed gently back. "Would you like a tour?"

"That would be lovely," Lois responded. With that we followed single file around the floating Five Star hotel. Nothing was spared; staterooms with floor-to-ceiling windows, a saloon leading to an upper deck balcony, the sun deck afforded a luxury spa. We ended on the upper deck and noticed we were motoring out to sea, the harbor a faint speck in the distance.

"We'll watch the sunset up here and then have dinner in the dining room."

As the boat cut through the choppy water effortlessly we were served hors d'oeuvres on silver platters. Shrimp cocktail, oysters Rockefeller, and caviar over triangular pieces of toast.

"What's this?" Amanda leaned over and asked me with a cracker in her hand topped with black caviar.

"Caviar," I said, not wanting her to be aghast at what it was.

"Fish eggs," Luke leaned in to tell her from my other side.

I reached over and nudged him with my arm as I watched her scrunch up her face in disgust. Sarah reached over and took it from her, "I'll eat it."

How much longer will we be able to afford this one, I wondered.

"If you watch the sun very closely as it sets just at the horizon line, you may be able to see what they call the green flash," Mr. Whittier walked over and told us, Isabel following. He pointed at the west and we watched fiercely as the sun dipped below the line between night and day but saw nothing. "Ah well, maybe another day." He turned back to us and reached his arm around Isabel bringing her into the conversation. "My lovely wife is from Brazil."

"What is Brazil like; we've never been?" I asked her.

"She doesn't speak English," Mr. Whittier replied, as she nodded her head.

"*Yo hablo un poquito español*," Sarah said to her.

With that, Isabel unleashed a fervent amount of words as fast as a gazelle running from a lion. When she poured out all she could in a sentence she stopped and waited for Sarah to reply.

"*Un poquito*," Sarah said as she held her hand up allowing just a tiny space between her thumb and index finger, "Just a little." Conversation over, Isabel slinked back.

"Her native language is Portuguese," Mr. Wittier corrected Sarah. "Brazilian Portuguese is similar to Spanish."

A waiter came up the stairs and announced, "Dinner is ready, sir."

The white linen tablecloth was adorned with two silver candelabras with glowing candles. In the center lay a flat contemporary floral arrangement filled with merlot-colored roses. We were each served a Caribbean lobster tail, julienned carrots and a twice-baked stuffed potato. My father helped carry the conversation through most of the meal. Amanda asked our host if he ever saw dolphins out in the ocean here. He told her there were pods of them and whales too, but it was too early in the season to see whales now.

When the plates were cleared, Mr. Whittier reached into his jacket and pulled out a cigar. "Anyone else?" My dad and Luke both cheered.

As Mr. Whittier lit his cigar he said to my father sitting at the other end of the table, "Turlington said he will meet us at the site tomorrow at eleven."

My father let out a puff of smoke, "Okay. I rented a Jeep like you said, I think it will take us about an hour to get over to that side of the island."

Turlington, that name sounded familiar. "Isn't that the gentlemen who bought up a lot of land here for preservation?" I asked. I think this was the guy Bane had told me about.

"That was Turlington Senior. We are meeting Turlington Junior. Old man Turlington died last year. He intended to put all the land into a trust for a preserve here in Triton, but he never finished the legal process, and died of a sudden heart attack. His son, thank God, has more sense. He's selling off the parcels for development. It will be good for the people here to get some real jobs instead of lying around under palm trees all day." Mr. Whittier took another puff of his cigar.

I sat in shock while I bit my tongue. The room was filling with sweet, heavy smoke. I could feel the girls looking at me. No doubt their eyes were starting to get irritated too.

"Yup, your dad and I are going to make a lot of money here. The hardest thing will be keeping those Haitians from trying to come over in their makeshift boats looking for a free handout." He let a cloud waft out of his mouth while I started wishing he would get lung cancer.

"Can I come with you?" I wanted to change the conversation. Bane had said that some of the most beautiful parts of the island were over on the south shore but they were hard to get to.

"We have two extra seats in the Jeep," my dad offered.

"Can I come too?" Amanda jumped in, always up for an adventure. I looked at Sarah and Luke.

"We made an appointment for pedicures at the spa tomorrow," Sarah shared as she looked over at Lois.

"I was thinking of going on the fishing expedition," Luke said. "Why don't you two go ahead."

"It's going to be a bumpy ride, rough terrain right now until we get a proper road over there, but you're welcome to come," Mr. Whittier said.

We didn't even bother to ask poor Isabel. She didn't look interested in going anywhere other than back to her Barbie castle.

I wanted to see exactly what my dad was getting himself into.

Chapter 50

AMANDA

We bounced back and forth like dice in the Yahtzee cup. The Jeep Granddad rented was really cool, kinda like the ones you see on African safari shows. Mom and I sat in the backseat, Granddad and Mr. Whittier in the front.

"We're almost there," Mr. Whittier shouted back to us. "Turn in there, William."

All we saw was the same thick shrubs lining the road ever since we turned off the main road, which seemed like several miles back. We passed only one other car, a Jeep too, which barely squeezed by us.

"The site is straight ahead." Mr. Whittier pointed.

As we got near the end of this last road, a path really, there were fewer shrubs and more patches of sand. Eventually it was just clusters of grass and then a big open clearing leading to sky blue sea. Black rugged rock formed a small mountain to the right of us; the left was clear sand as far as the eye could see.

"Beautiful, ain't it?" Mr. Whittier said as Granddad turned off the ignition.

"Sure is," Granddad replied.

Mom got out of the car and marveled. "I didn't think this island could get any more beautiful."

The adults stood together talking while I walked down to the water. A squadron of pelicans swooped down and skimmed across the ocean. I shuffled through the sand, then yelled back to my mom, "I'm going to see what's on top of there," angling toward the top of the massive rock.

She followed me. "Wait! I'll go with you."

"What kind of rock is this?" I asked as we began scaling our way to the top. The rock was jagged with lots of pockets and some pools filled with water and sea urchins.

"It's probably an old coral reef," she said as she paused to rest for a second on a plateau.

I ventured forward and reached the pinnacle first. "Wow!"

Mom scurried to catch up to me. "Wow is right."

Below us was a fully enclosed pool except for a small bridge in the deep end that connected to the sea.

"It's like a swimming pool."

"Let's go in it," I said as I climbed down toward it before she could object.

"Wait for me," she squealed.

As soon as I hit sand again, I peeled my clothes off, glad that we had decided to wear our bathing suits, just in case. The water in the pool was peaceful and still.

"This is really special." Mom seemed just as excited as I was.

Together we waded in and paddled out, our feet no longer touching the bottom.

"I wish we brought our snorkels, we could swim right

under that bridge and see what's out there," I said as I got close to a bridge in the rock.

"Be careful, let's not go too close to that, there may be a current and there are no lifeguards here."

I clung to the edge and peered through the bridge at the endless ocean. Small crabs scurried in and out of holes near my fingers.

A loud warbling squawk captured our attention; it got louder and louder. We weren't alone.

Mom grabbed the rock next to me. "Do you hear that?"

"How can I not? What do you think it is?"

The sound, although unknown to our ears, sounded like a loud group of farm animals.

"I don't know," she said as she listened intently.

"It sounds like it is coming from the other side of that big rock," I pointed to the side we had not yet explored. "Let's go see," and to my surprise Mom followed behind me.

We put our sneakers back on and climbed the rock in our wet bathing suits, slowly, side by side. As we neared the top, the sound got louder. Cautiously, we peered over the top like we were in an adventure movie, my heart pounded. I let her peer over the top first. She smiled and stood on top of the rock. I followed her lead.

"Are those flamingos?" I squealed in delight.

"I think so, a flamboyance of them."

Relieved, we stood and admired the huge mass of pink, squawking at each other, ignoring us. They lined the entire shoreline and waded in the shallow water created by a sandbar.

"They're beautiful. Can we go down there?" I looked at Mom.

"No, honey, I think it's best if we just look from here. We don't want to disrupt them. I don't know that much about flamingos."

I didn't know much about them either so I didn't fight her on this one. We sat and just enjoyed watching them.

"Granddad! There are flamingos over there, hundreds of them." I ran over to the men who were huddled together with some other guys.

"Anton, this is my granddaughter, Amanda, and my daughter, Jill." He pointed at Mom who was still meandering toward us.

"Nice to meet you, young lady," he said. I was glad he didn't hold his hand out for me to shake.

"That area over there, we plan to make it into a dock and boathouse," Mr. Whittier spoke like I wasn't there. He looked over toward where I had just come from. "We'll bulldoze that rock, dredge the area."

"But what about the flamingos?" I cried.

"They'll find a new home," he shrugged.

"But you have to see it; there is even a cool part that is just like a swimming pool!"

Mom walked up and looked at me, then at the men. "Hello."

"Mom, they are going to turn that into a dock," I exclaimed, horrified as I grabbed her arm to make sure she was listening.

Mr. Whittier stood impatiently. The new man stood with his arms crossed and Granddad got the stern look on his face that meant he was probably going to yell. Instead he said, "Why don't you two wait in the Jeep, we're almost done here."

Mom pulled me away from the men and led me back to the Jeep. "But they're going to bulldoze all that!" I said.

Mom and I didn't say a word the whole way back. I could only catch parts of the conversation Mr. Whittier was having with Granddad; hotel ten stories, endless pool, golf course, tennis. Mom rubbed her chin repeatedly.

When we got to Mr. Whittier's boat, he got out without saying goodbye to us. Mom got shotgun.

When Mr. Whittier was out of earshot, my mother asked Granddad, "What exactly are you planning on creating out there?"

Granddad waited until he pulled out of the parking lot before replying. "Don't you EVER talk like that while I am having a business meeting." His head turned quickly, looked straight at me, then back to the road.

"Don't talk to her like that!" Mom shouted back in my defense. "You don't even know what's there but you're ready to bulldoze it all down?"

"You can be such a hypocrite, Jill," he grumbled.

"Hypocrite, I'm not a hypocrite. I'm just saying that there is a lot of wildlife out there. Shouldn't you go and assess it before you destroy what you may not be able to get back?"

"That takes money, Jill. Money, you know the stuff that put a roof over our heads all these years, the stuff that sent you to college, that helped you with the down payment on that farmhouse you wanted."

I wanted to jump in and point out that they could destroy the sea turtles that lay eggs on quiet beaches like that, but now probably wasn't the right time. Granddad looked like steam could blow out of his ears any minute and Mom was fidgeting in her seat so much I wondered if she might just jump out.

No one said another word. The tension was giving me stomach pains. When we finally got to the resort, Mom leapt from the Jeep, opened my door and commanded me to get out. She whisked me away, leaving Granddad boiling.

Chapter 51

JILL

We ate Thanksgiving dinner by ourselves that night; Luke, Sarah, Amanda and me. The girls were quiet. The resort's buffet was filled with traditional American Thanksgiving Day food, even though it wasn't a holiday they celebrated on the island. Dad and Lois were nowhere in sight. This wasn't the blissful getaway that I had in mind.

Luke listened to me, patiently as usual, as I ranted about how my father was going to be part of a group determined to destroy the virgin nature on the island. My husband was used to being the sounding board when it came to the friction between my dad and me.

Things were never this volatile between us when my mother was alive. Then again, we rarely talked in a real meaningful way just he and I. I never realized how much my mother played the role of conductor in our family. She knew just how to maneuver our lives so we played like a symphony. She was our anchor. She was our confidante, our information broker. She shared the goings-on in our lives between us as we each lived our separate lives. Without her we drifted, lost at sea.

"I hear you; I wish more people would consider the impact that their actions have on the environment, Jill. But your dad has a point. You've enjoyed a lot of things in your life because he's provided them to you. He has a right to make his own decisions."

I hated when Luke tried to get me to understand my father's side. I wanted him to say, "That's awful, I'll go knock his lights out." Okay, well maybe not to that extreme, but at least take my side. He had a way though of being a fire extinguisher.

I wasn't ready to admit defeat yet. Instead I let my anger simmer, while I plotted my next move.

I awoke first, peeked at the clock, 6:35 a.m. Luke gently snored beside me. Slowly, I slipped out of the bed, picked a pair of shorts and a T-shirt out of my luggage and got dressed in the bathroom.

My face glowed with fresh color, my hair looked shinier. I brushed my teeth, and then scribbled a quick note, which I left by the sink in case Luke awoke before I got back.

Went for a walk on the beach ☺ 6:35. If I'm not back when you all awake, go to breakfast without me. I didn't want to feel pressured by time this morning.

A couple jogged ahead of me down to the beach, leaving their footprints for me to follow. They went east, so I chose to walk west. I needed my own space to think, clear my head.

It must have rained last night, I thought. The beach was moist. As I looked back at the palm trees behind me I saw a rainbow fade away. The words that sang in my head during my initial visit to Triton played again.

I know you're there
By the rainbows I see.
I know you're there,
Watching over me.
I know you're there by the sound of the crow,
I know you're there, I know you're there.

Good timing, Mom, I thought to myself. I felt comforted that she may very well be vacationing with us too.

Shuffling step by step along the water's edge the sea washed intermittently over my feet. What is it about the beach? Is it the simplicity of just sand, big open sky and the vast ocean? Does the sea, void of all the visual chaos in our urban and suburban lives, allow our mind's space to unclutter itself? Whatever it was, I was soaking it in.

In the distance, a lone hammock gently rocked like a cradle alone in between dunes of sand and sea grass. Two sturdy towering palm trees held it up.

As I got closer it seemed to beckon me, "Come lie down, kick your feet up." I resisted the urge at first, but then thought better of it. Why not, my note didn't specify a time when I would return.

I steadied the web of rope and shimmied back and forth to find a spot where my weight might be best distributed. I nearly tumbled on the first try but mastered it on the second when I planted my butt deep in the center and rolled the rest of me in until I was fully and firmly cradled.

The palms up above filtered the sun's rays. And there I lay, and lay, listening to the repetitive roar of the ocean thrusting itself on shore like a bottle of uncorked champagne on New Year's Eve. Over and over the sea dribbled up the sand leaving foaming mounds of bubbles until it was called back home. Then it slid back calmly into the abyss.

The droned on chatter in my head droned on: what do I do about my father now? Is this trip helping Amanda? Why is it so hard for me to get through to Sarah? I wanted this trip to be fun. Did I bring enough sunscreen? All of those clamoring thoughts vying for my attention evaporated until my mind was as silent as the school hallways once all the kids went home. I didn't realize how long I basked in the stillness until it was abruptly interrupted.

"Mom, you said I could use the boogie board first." A girl with pigtails wearing a plum purple bathing suit stood at the edge of the boardwalk that led from the nearby hotel to the beach, her hands on each of her hips. A boy a little taller ran onto the sand with the boogie board tightly grasped under his arm. I shot the little girl my best I'm warning you glance. She caught it but turned away appearing unfazed and repeated her whiny cry, this time louder, "Mom!"

The young boy peeled off his clothes and darted into the waves.

"Roger, I told you to wait for me," a woman's voice bellowed but I didn't see the body it belonged to. Roger was atop the boogie board now, belly down, gliding along the top of the waves until they parked him on the sand.

A young mother, loaded up like a donkey with a small cooler, beach bag, and towels, tried to juggle the two pairs of kids' sandals in her hands as she wiped her brow. My frustration turned to gratitude; thank goodness my own girls have grown out of that stage. They were cute when they were cute, but when they weren't, oh boy.

"Mom, tell him to give it to me," the young girl wailed again.

"Roger," the mom yelled out in vain.

Maybe it was time for me to move on anyway, I rolled until the hammock threatened to toss me on the ground, then hurled my feet over and stood up. The sun was sizzling now. Maybe I should just get this over with.

There wasn't a soul in the water yet as I meandered down the beach toward the real estate development office. People were starting to claim beach chairs with their towels and I had more walking company. I stopped to gaze for a moment at the vast blue wonderland beside me. Scanning back and forth with my hand, I shaded my eyes I hoped to see a dorsal fin.

"You probably won't see him this morning, not down this far," a man's voice startled me.

The voice belonged to an older guy, maybe in his late sixties, gray hair, gray beard, wearing tan cargo shorts and a T-shirt with some kind of fishing tournament emblem over his heart. His skin was leathered from the sun, his eyes a soft shade of blue.

"Sharky, right? That's who you're looking for?" he added.

"How did you know?" I let my arm rest to my side and

turned towards him.

"I know that look of longing," he chuckled a bit.

"So, you know Sharky? How do you know he won't be out here," I pointed straight out to the sea.

"I saw him this morning down the east side of the bay while I was fishing," he pointed in the direction I had walked from. "The water activities will start soon and he'll probably get distracted by them and hang out up there. The water is pretty smooth today so he won't be so anxious to go to the other side of the island or further out to sea."

"It sounds like you know him pretty well." I was intrigued.

"You could say that," he said with a tone of reflection.

"Do you live here?"

"I do now, used to live in New York."

"That's where I'm from," I said somewhat excited that we shared a connection. "How did you get down here?"

"It's a long story, but the short version is I was one of the surviving firefighters of 9/11. I was within a half block of the towers when they started to collapse. Being a New Yorker, I don't have to tell you all the grim details." He paused, looked at me and my heart sank.

I shook my head no. No, he didn't have to tell me the details. I remember them all too clearly even though I watched it unfold live on a television screen. That was bad enough.

"A friend of mine suggested that I come down here a few months after that. I was in a pretty dark place."

I stayed silent and waited for him to continue.

"I was out taking a swim one morning and Sharky

scared the hell out of me," his tone lightened up and I smiled knowingly. "He came right up to me. I'm surprised I didn't have a heart attack."

"I know, he did that to me too the first time I came down here," I added.

"Well, once I figured out it was a dolphin I stopped and caught my breath. He waited there, right next to me. I couldn't believe it. So I started swimming again and he swam right alongside me. He kept doing his clicking noises, echolocation. It was a life altering moment."

A spark lit inside me. Maybe this guy knows that feeling, that feeling I got from Sharky when I swam with him. Would he think I was crazy if I asked him? I needed to know. "Can I ask you something?"

"Sure," he nodded.

"When you swam with Sharky, did you feel different? Not just different, but amazing, euphoric almost?"

"Absolutely!" he responded to my surprise.

"Really." Now I wanted to know more.

"Not just while I was swimming with him but for days afterward," he seemed just as excited to talk to someone who understood the feeling as I was.

"Yes, exactly. Why is that, do you suppose?"

"I know there are a lot of people who think it's a mystical thing, spiritual all this kind of nonsense. I believe it has to do with his sonar. The question then becomes is the dolphin doing it intentionally or does the sonar's effect on us just happen as he is doing his normal scanning activity?" He let his hands rest in his pockets now.

Sonar, I thought to myself. Look at what lithotripsy does

for kidney stones. The ultrasonic waves can blast just the stones and they disintegrate so the patient can pass them on their own when they urinate. It was a revolutionary way to avoid a major surgery to remove the stones. Maybe the sonar works on the human emotions the way crystal sonic therapy works. Just by listening to two different frequencies of sound, the mind blends them in to one, leaving the patient with a feeling of calm. My mind was racing!

"The problem is," he continued on, interrupting my thoughts. "People come down here and chase after the dolphin. Some are just stupid; they jump off the boats and try to ride him. Others come down and scout him out specifically thinking he can heal them."

Gulp. Guilty.

"There are all these stories that he swims alone and likes to interact with humans. But I think that he is just being a dolphin. I think this bay is his bedroom, a place where he can catch a nap without worrying about being attacked by sharks. And I know he doesn't just hang out by himself. There is a whole pod out there he hangs with. I'm pretty sure some of the babies I've seen are his. He stays very close to the mother and calf when they are young."

"So why do you think he swims with people?" I asked.

He chuckled. "Curiosity. Good old-fashioned curiosity. Imagine waking up from a nap and noticing something in your bedroom. Wouldn't you go and check it out?"

"Makes sense to me," I agreed. The sun was beginning to feel scorching.

This man must have felt it too because he looked up and squinted at the sun. "Well, I've got to get back before lunch. I usually do my brisk walk in the morning before it gets too hot. My name is Frank, by the way." He held his hand out.

"Jill," I shook his hand then let go. "It has been a real pleasure speaking with you, Frank."

"Likewise," he said as he took another peek at the sun. "Enjoy your stay."

As he marched away, I looked back at the open ocean. What an amazing research project it would be to see if the sonar that dolphins use could be used to help people heal from grief, traumatic stress, and depression. Surely the navy must know the frequencies by now. What if it could be put into a device? Before I let my mind run off any further on this tangent, I stopped. And when would I have time to do this? Why does life offer too many choices and not enough time?

Chapter 52

AMANDA

The sound of Sarah blow drying her hair woke me up out of a sound sleep. Arrgh! Dad knocked on the door that adjoined our rooms.

"Come in," I yelled.

"Ready for breakfast?"

"What time is it?" I asked as I wiped my eyes.

"Ten after eight."

I sat up and stretched my arms to the ceiling. "Okay, I just need a minute to get dressed."

The scream of the hairdryer stopped. Sarah came out of the bathroom in a cheery mood for a change, "Good morning, Dad."

I peered in my parents' room before I headed into the bathroom. "Where's Mom?"

"She went for a walk."

She must really be pissed or upset, that's when she goes for long walks. I wasn't feeling so cheery myself. Grandpa didn't seem to care that he was going to ruin where those flamingos live. And today was Friday; we only had two more days for me to find Sharky again.

As we walked toward the restaurant, my teeth minty fresh, I asked, "Can we go paddleboarding today?"

"Lois and I are going to the spa," Sarah said.

"I guess so, why not?" Dad said to me.

Mom never showed up for breakfast so we left. Sarah went off to meet Lois at the spa and I rushed Dad down to the sports shack. Laird was there, putting snorkels together with masks.

"Ready for some more adventure, are you?" he asked.

"We want to paddleboard again," I said looking up to him.

"Have you snorkeled yet?"

I looked back at my dad who replied, "No, haven't tried that."

"We have a boat going out to the reef in ten minutes if you want to give it a go?"

I was torn. Mom said the snorkeling is amazing, but I didn't want to miss Sharky.

"She wants to see the dolphin again," Dad answered as he put his hand on my shoulder.

"You have just as good a chance to see him out there as on a paddleboard. Maybe even more so, he usually hunts for fish in the morning."

"What do you say?" Dad asked me.

"Let's try snorkeling."

Laird fit us up with masks, snorkels and fins. He gave us some tips and sent us to catch the small boat pulled ashore in front of us. Another couple waited to board, armed with the same equipment.

A native islander introduced himself as Ollie. He pushed

the boat out until it was floating and we all waded out and climbed the ladder into it. He revved the engine and we were off.

The couple sat across from us and gave a little wave hello. The engine was too loud to try and talk. The front of the boat tilted up. We each grabbed our seats a little tighter as our hair flew in a hundred different directions. I looked back and watched the shore grow smaller and smaller until it was just barely visible. Then the engine stopped and the boat settled down into the waves.

"It's a little choppier out here because this is where the waves break over the reef," Ollie informed us. "We are going to stay on this side of the reef, where it's calmer."

Ollie went over the same tips that Laird told us. Spit in your mask so it stays clear. Remember to blow out hard to clear your snorkel once we are in the water. Make sure you don't pull the mask up and let it sit on your head. Relax.

We let the other couple go first. Then Dad got in. Then me.

For a minute I felt panicky when all I could see was bubbles around me and I couldn't breathe. But once the water cleared all I could say was, "Wow!"

I blew hard on my snorkel and sucked in a gulp of air. From then on, I didn't even have to think about breathing. Dad looked back to see if I was near him, I waved. There were fish everywhere! In front of us, below us, I turned around and they were there too. Big fish, small fish, yellow with blue strips, bright blue with green and red, long, skinny silver ones. Oh wait until Rachel and Kailey hear about this.

Dad stopped and pointed below. A mound of coral sat just a foot away from us. Inside a crevice was a lobster hiding. As we bobbed on the surface, purple sea fans swayed on the coral further down. Anemone waved their tentacles. Fish pecked at the coral. It was a whole other world, one that I wondered about from above the waves.

Dad waved me on and I followed. I saw a fish that looked like Dory but no Nemo. And no Sharky.

We weaved our way through the coral like we were flying through canyons. A giant crab scrambled to hide from us and then I spotted a puffer fish. I kicked faster so I could grab Dad's leg. I think I scared him because he turned around really quick and his eyes were wide open in his mask. I pointed quickly down below us. The puffer fish flapped its little fins and flew away. On the ocean floor a fish lay still, just like a rock. A huge school of bright yellow fish with blue tinged eyes swam right by us. We stopped and let them pass.

Dad pointed his finger towards the surface and poked his head out. I followed. We pulled our masks down around our necks and took our snorkels out of our mouths.

"Pretty cool, huh?" Dad said wiping his eyes.

"Very cool," I agreed. As I kicked my legs below to keep afloat, I looked around for Sharky. Nothing. We were pretty far from the boat though.

"I think we should head back. We don't want to get too far away," He said pointing towards the boat. Ollie stood on top, keeping an eye out for where we were. He waved us to come closer.

We spit in our masks, rubbed the plastic with our

fingers, rinsed them and then let them suck onto our faces.

"Ready?"

I nodded yes and put my snorkel in my mouth. Back into the underwater world we went. There were too many different types of fish to count. I could hear the waves rush along my ears and my breath via the snorkel. Otherwise it was silent. No talking, no honking, no dogs barking, no TV. It was like all the creatures we saw just knew how to live together without saying a word.

Up ahead, I could see the white hull of the boat. I didn't want to get back in. I turned to head the other way. As I did, I felt a ZIZZZ feeling. It ripped through my whole body. It stopped. Then it happened again, more intense this time, ZIZZZ. It was a cool feeling, almost like when your finger is a little wet and you plug something in. Then I saw him, Sharky.

He swam faster than I did and dipped below me. Then he left. I heard nothing, I couldn't see him. Then I felt it again, ZIZZZ. This time he came closer. He stayed on top of the water. I swam closer to him. We looked eye to eye.

ZIZZZ. He tilted his head the way Peaches does.

I garbled, "Hi, Sharky," through my snorkel.

ZIZZZ.

He swam slowly. I kicked gently and followed alongside of him. My two eyes stared into his one. I reached my hand out slowly to touch him. He was so close. I stopped when his jaw started opening and closing fast. He looked annoyed; I pulled my hand back and his mouth closed. He looked like he was smiling. I knew though, that is just how dolphins look all the time. Their mouths are made that way.

It didn't matter. He seemed happy to me. I couldn't be any happier.

I could hear water splashing hard behind me. I turned and saw my dad thrashing, paddling hard trying to catch up to me. Sharky sped off. I stopped and popped my head out of the water. I was pretty far away from the boat again. Everyone else except for us was on it.

Dad stopped and threw his head up and ripped his mask off. "You're getting too far," he took a couple of breaths, "from the boat."

"Did you see Sharky," I shouted. I could be a real mermaid. Life is so much better out here.

"Yes, we were watching," he waved me towards him. "But, we need to go back."

I scanned the waves around me. Sharky was gone. I didn't want my dad to drown. He looked like he was getting tired.

"Okay," I said quietly.

We paddled back to the boat. Reluctantly I got back in. I felt amazing.

Chapter 53

JILL

I opened the door of the real estate office and found Mr. Whittier talking to the office secretary.

"I'm sorry to interrupt, I was just looking for my father," I said.

Mr. Whittier handed a pile of papers to the secretary and waved me in. "He's not here at the moment but come in." His wave was insistent so I followed his command. "Sylvia, could you make us some coffee?"

He placed his hand on my upper back and motioned me toward a room lit brightly with a large table in the center. "Your father went to get some lunch, he should be back shortly. Have you seen the plans for our resort?"

I pulled back, like a dog on a leash that wants to stop to take a sniff of a nearby tree. No, I hadn't seen the plans and quite frankly I didn't want to see them. The last thing I wanted to do was get in a position of conflict with this man.

Sensing my reluctance, he added, "We've been working all morning putting the finishing touches on the new plan."

New plan? My father didn't mention anything about a

new plan, But then again, we hadn't spoken since the trip out to the site. I slowly headed for the large design table.

"This section over here will all be single residence rentals, all one level. There will be a communal dining area with a hydroponic greenhouse attached to it. The entire development will be green friendly-solar powered electric, with rain catchment systems. We're working on the sewage treatment, and have two different proposals."

I looked down at the architectural sketches. The resort was lush, loaded with indigenous trees and shrubs.

"I don't understand, I thought you were going to construct big high-rise hotels and have a swim with the dolphin waterpark?"

"Well, our senior architect flew in late yesterday. He recently attended an international resort development conference, thank goodness. He came up with a better plan. He asked us, 'Is this really what people are going to want to pay to travel here for? Why not go to their local theme park?' No, he said the way the global population is building and natural resources are being destroyed, we would be much better in the long haul if we created a place that was different from where people in urban areas live. We should make this a place to escape to, unplug, where you can hear yourself think again. Where families can talk, create their own fun, play games. It will be pricier, but it will be special."

Nearly a third of the plan was void of buildings. Pathways lead to a labyrinth. An area was labeled "Helen's Hideaway." I gently led my finger around the labyrinth.

"Your father was stubborn as a goat on that part. We

didn't want to give up all that acreage for just a natural park. He insisted though and the partners only gave in when he offered to foot the bill for that acreage of the project. He named it Helen's Hideaway after your mother. Said she was always retreating out to nature to keep her sanity. He said that was probably what allowed her to put up with him as long as she did." Mr. Whittier chuckled like it was funny as he rolled back on his heels.

My throat clenched tight and I smiled along with Mr. Whittier so I wouldn't cry. I had no idea what made my father take such a one hundred and eighty degree turn, but I wasn't going to argue with it.

I heard my father's voice coming closer, "Yes, lunch was terrific, thank you for the recommendation, Sylvia."

He entered the design room but stopped abruptly when he saw me. He shuffled back a step. He looked at me, then the plans on the table, then back at me.

"Ahh, William. I was just showing Jill here the new plans."

My father stood silent, as if bracing for an attack.

I walked over and stood on my toes and kissed him on the cheek.

* * *

As soon as I saw Amanda I knew something had changed in her. She was bubbly, exuberant, playing volleyball in the pool with Luke. They laughed and giggled and splashed each other like little kids. My heart swooned.

When she saw me she nearly leapt out of the pool and

ran over.

"Mom! You're not going to believe this! We went snorkeling and Sharky swam right up to me." She held her hands up together shaking them. "We swam together for a long time."

Luke shook the water off himself and concurred with her story.

The conversation with Frank this morning replayed itself. The last thing I wanted to do was squelch Amanda's enthusiasm and joy. This is what I wanted, wasn't it? At the same time, I didn't want to hurt the dolphin.

"That's terrific, Amanda." I said proudly. "You didn't chase after him, did you?"

"No, Mom, that's the best part, he came up and surprised me." Her smile was so bright I needed sunglasses to look at her.

"Yeah, we watched from the boat," Luke added. "They hung out together for a good while. Then he swam off."

Amanda turned and gave her dad a stern look while she crossed her arms.

"Okay, so I may have scared him off when I swam out to them. But she was getting too far away from the boat," he patted Amanda on the head.

I hugged Amanda then held her shoulders and looked at her. "How do you feel?"

"Amazing," she stamped her foot. "Like I have never been so happy in my whole entire life!"

Interesting, I thought to myself. "I'm happy for you. Let's just remember, though, that he is a wild dolphin. We don't chase after them."

She rolled her eyes at me like I was the dumb one. I've gotten used to that lately. "Where's Sarah?"

"She might be back in the room," Luke answered.

"I'll go check on her," I said.

They ran and jumped back in the pool.

A warm tropical breeze delivered a floral scent as I slid our key into the lock. Finally, I felt like we are on vacation.

"Where have you been?" Sarah bellowed at me.

"Why? What's wrong?" The bliss inside me evaporated and my shoulders clenched with worry.

"I got my period and they ran out of tampons in the gift store. They won't be getting another delivery until next week. I can't wear these diaper things!" She reached up and pulled at her hair.

"Okay, okay. I will take a taxi to the local grocery store and see if they have them. Do you want to come?"

"No! I'm not going anywhere like this," she turned away and went in the other room.

So much for sitting at the beach. I grabbed my purse and headed for the front desk.

Chapter 54

AMANDA

The volleyball sailed over my head. There was no way I could reach it. I swam to the edge of the pool to get it. Granddad and Lois walked over to the edge.

"Having fun?" Lois asked.

"Yeah, but Dad is beating me," I grabbed the ball and wiped my face.

"Where's your mother?" Granddad asked.

I was too happy to be mad at him now. I shrugged. "I think she went to the room to find Sarah."

Dad paddled over to join us.

"William made arrangements with the restaurant staff to have a private dinner set up for all of us tonight," Lois announced. She looked over at Granddad. He turned and looked out at the ocean.

It kind of sucked having Thanksgiving by ourselves last night.

"Thank you," Dad said. "What time, where? I'll tell Jill. I'm sure she will be excited."

"Six o'clock. Let's meet in front of the main dining room," Lois informed us.

"Sounds like a plan," Dad confirmed.

"Want to come in and play?" I asked.

They both looked at me, Granddad smirked.

"Thank you, honey, but we are going to go for a walk on the beach and maybe take a nap before dinner," Lois said as she reached out for Granddad's hand.

"Okay," I said, then grabbed my dad. "Come on, I'm going to beat you!"

Chapter 55

JILL

The trip to the only grocery store on the island required a taxi. Darly arranged a ride for me with the old Datsun taxi that happened to be waiting for a customer. A thin man, with a front tooth missing, sat in the driver's seat. I wondered if he too were a descendant of the African slaves brought to the island years ago to create salt, but didn't ask.

The car was missing its shock absorbers. I didn't say anything, hoping it would allow him to concentrate on his driving. We made it in one piece and he pulled right up to the front door to let me out.

"Would you mind waiting?" I asked.

"Yes, yes, I wait right over there." He swung his arm to a space on the far side of the parking lot where a tree offered shade.

"Thank you," the door cried as I closed it. "I'll just be a minute."

He cut across the spaces and headed directly to the spot.

The grocery store greeted me with a wall of tropical fruit all stacked in wooden crates; pineapples, mangoes, bananas, and a few that I couldn't even name. I asked the only woman at the cash register where the feminine products were. She wrinkled her forehead and tilted her head. "Tampons," I said softly.

"Oh, they over there in Aisle Three." she pointed where I should go.

"Thank you."

I scurried over to Aisle Three and searched the shelves. Pampers, and baby wipes, were mixed with Lysol, mops, and Windex in the next row. An arm reached for a roll of paper towels. I glanced over to see whom it belonged to and nearly fainted. He put the roll of paper towels in the basket he carried and reached for another. I couldn't help but stare. His resemblance was so striking. Dark black hair, dark sculpted eyebrows, tan skin, but he was taller. He looked at me and tossed me a friendly smile. His eyes were the same.

I just stood with my mouth open and stared. He moseyed along. He was about Amanda's age, maybe a little younger. He looked like a young version of Enrique Iglesias.

When he turned out of the aisle, I sped up to follow him. As I passed the tampons, I grabbed a box and scrambled to the next aisle looking for him. I could see he was already in line to pay for his groceries. The female cashier waved him over to her open register. A mother with three kids and a cart full of groceries got in line behind him.

Dammit.

The next best option was the young guy on the end who was half finished ringing his customer. I got in that line and gawked at the boy. The female cashier gushed while she bagged the teen's purchases. He helped her bag them up.

Aww, he's helpful too.

"How are you today?" my cashier was jubilant, but a scrawny thing. At least he moved quickly. The boy was paying.

"Great, thank you." I grabbed a bag and threw the tampons in and threw ten dollars at the cashier. The boy was leaving. "Keep the change."

Two older ladies clogged the exit with their chitchat just as I got there.

"Haven't seen you in a while."

"My breathing not so good. I taking it easy."

"Excuse me, please." I forced a smile and they let me through.

As fast as I could I ran over to the taxi. The driver had the window rolled down and his head lay back on the headrest. His eyes closed.

"I'm ready!" I shouted from fifty feet away, hoping to wake him up.

As I got closer to the car, I repeated myself louder.

He slowly opened his eyes and rubbed them.

Before I could close the door I was already barking at him, "Can we follow that kid on a bike?" I pointed as he was just pulling out onto the main road quickly.

The driver looked back at me and shook his head ever so slightly. Without a word he started the engine. If he knew who the guy in the boy on the bike was, he didn't say anything. The engine grinded then stopped. The driver sat up straighter and leaned in towards the steering wheel and turned the key again. Reluctantly it started.

"Gotta give it a minute," he said without looking back.

I felt my muscles tense and I strained to see the boy almost out of sight.

I heard the click of the shaft being put into drive and we were off. Once we hit the main road, the driver hit the gas. I held on to the seat and the door handle tight. The bag of tampons bounced down to the floor. I could see the boy again far ahead. Another taxi rode between us. It was full and we were riding on its tail before we knew it.

"Ugh," I whispered loudly.

My driver took a peek in the rearview mirror then he peered around the taxi and floored it. He weaved around the other taxi and sped up just in time to see the boy making a turn. He slowed down again. Then the boy made the same turn into the same dock area that Whittier's boat was docked in.

The boy hopped off his bike and leaned his bike against a fence near a two-story dive boat.

"Stop, please." I leaned over and tapped the driver. He slammed on the brakes. Taxis were coming in and out of the boatyard. I would take my chances.

"Thank you so much." I handed the driver a twenty dollar bill. His smile said it had been worth the while.

With my bag of tampons in hand, I got out and stood and stared as the boy went below deck of the dive boat. On the upper deck a middle-aged man with scraggly hair fiddled with a rope. His bare chest was lean but not muscular. His long khaki shorts were well worn.

I inched my way closer. Then I saw him. Standing on the dock, tying a buoy onto the side of the boat. His dark hair was now salt and pepper colored. The skin on his arms and face still tanned but weathered. He stood up and stretched while reaching an arm back towards his spine. I know that feeling after you've bent down too long. He turned and caught me staring. For a split second I thought about running in the opposite direction and grabbing a cab. My feet wouldn't move and my eyes met his.

He had the same dark eyebrows that the boy had. They squished together. His mouth dropped. I fumbled to put a smile on my face. I reached up and started rubbing my neck with my hand nervously. Then I nodded my head, yes. *Yes, it's me.*

We walked toward each other slowly. I stopped at the edge of the dock and let him come to me.

"Jill?"

"Yes."

"I'm in shock." Bane stood and just looked at me up and down.

"I'm pretty surprised to see you too," I said.

"What brings you here?"

"Vacation. And my dad is thinking of doing some investing here." I waved my hand in the air.

"Wow, it's been a long time."

Then, as the awkward surprise wore off, we wrapped our arms around each other. "It's so good to see you."

He still felt muscular, but not as sculpted. The cotton T-shirt was moist with fresh sweat. He smelled raw with a hint of fresh showering from hours before.

We let each other go and I noticed the man on the upper deck had stopped toying with the rope and was now staring at us. Bane turned and shouted to him, "Remember Jill?"

The guy waved slowly.

I waved back.

"Remember Mason?" Bane asked me.

"Mason? Was he one of the guys you lived with?"

"Yes. We own this dive boat together now." Bane's chest puffed out as he pointed to the ship named *Another World*.

"It's a beauty, like the name." I brought my hands together.

"Yeah, business has been good. We're looking into getting another one." He looked back at Mason who was still staring. Mason returned his attention to the rope.

An awkward silence fell between us. We fidgeted like the kids at school waiting on line to go to the bathroom.

"You didn't go back to Hawaii?" I asked gently. For a moment I felt like we were the only two people on the island. The same way it felt like when we spent time on secluded beaches here years ago.

Bane looked down at the ground; he kicked a small rock to the side. "Yeah, but things didn't really work out the way I hoped they would."

"I'm sorry."

"Yeah, me too. I tried for a couple of years. My mom was happy to see me. She got cancer and passed away. I was glad that I got to spend those last moments with her."

"I'm sorry," I said again, while feeling a synergistic pain of grief. Remembering him saying that he hoped to have a better relationship with his dad, I asked, "Things work out with your dad?"

He shook his head no. "I tried."

"Hey, Dad, do you know where the extra hose is?" The boy emerged from below the boat and shouted out to us. He cocked his head when he saw me.

I just smiled.

"It's down below, under the sink," Bane yelled back.

The boy stood and watched us for a minute. When Bane turned back to me he went back below.

"You have a son," I said relieved the conversation had found a new direction.

"Yes, Kai, he's a good kid," he said with bashful pride. "Are you married? Kids?"

"Yes and yes, two girls," I pulled my phone out and showed him the photo that I saved on the front. Luke and the girls all grouped together for a selfie.

"Good looking family," Bane held the phone and gazed. "I bet your husband has to beat the boys off with a bat!"

I chuckled and added, "I bet that son of yours is a heartbreaker! Just like you." As soon as I said the words I regretted it.

Bane's face turned serious. "Jill, I thought about following you to New York. Really I did."

I held my hand up. This isn't what I was looking for. I wasn't sure what I was thinking coming here. "No, really, you don't have to explain."

"I feel I do. You see." He paused, took a deep breath. "I'm gay."

"Gay!" I felt my eyes open wide and my head lunge forward.

Bane recoiled and took a step back.

I reached my hand out and held his arm. "Gay?" I said softly this time.

He didn't say anything. I started giggling. Then laughing. He looked bewildered. The laughter became contagious.

"You think it's funny?" he asked.

"No, no," I held my stomach and let go of his arm. "I'm sorry, it's just that ever since I booked this trip I wondered what it would be like if I saw you again. Stupid me, I was thinking what would I do if we still had a spark?"

"Well, there's no spark that way, but I am glad to see you, Jill. I did, I do really care about you. The week we spent together meant a lot to me. You gave me the strength to go back to Hawaii." He paused. "I tried. I really tried to be straight." He held both hands in the air and flicked two fingers signaling quotation marks. "The hardest thing was telling my dad. I knew he wasn't going to take it well. He called me all kinds of names, I'm sure you can imagine. My mother wasn't surprised at all. In fact, she said, 'I always knew you were special.' When she died I couldn't stay there anymore."

Curious, I pointed to the boat. "So?"

"Kai?"

I nodded yes. Things were beginning to make sense. An empty hole in me pleasantly filled with answers to my lingering questions. At the same time, I felt relief. *Imagine if I had stayed longer during my first visit to try and make this relationship work.*

"Mason," Bane turned and pointed at Mason then turned back to me. "We're both business and life partners.

We wanted a child. A friend of ours on the island agreed to be a surrogate for us."

"That's terrific," I exclaimed.

Behind me the sound of cars driving across the gravel parking lot invaded our interlude. Doors began to slam. I took a quick peek behind me.

"We have a dive group going out in a few minutes," Bane said.

My heart felt like it shrank inside me. I didn't know what to say and at the same time I had so much to say, more questions to ask. I wanted a little more time.

"Would you like to get together later? How long are you on the island?"

An image of my family waiting for me back at the resort flashed before my eyes. Sarah was going to be furious with me for taking so long. "We leave the day after tomorrow. I'm afraid that I need to spend the short time that we have left with my family. I'm so glad we got to see each other though, Bane."

"Me too," he said as he leaned over and hugged me again.

I felt my twenty-four-year-old self become forty-one again. "Your father doesn't know what he's missing," I whispered in his ear and hugged him harder.

"Thanks," he whispered back.

Chapter 56

JILL

All of us met for breakfast on the Bistro deck that directly overlooked the ocean, minus my dad who went to play an early round of golf with his real estate buddies. We were all showing signs of getting into the slow, easy going rhythm of the island. Luke no longer looked at his watch every half hour, Sarah no longer threw her aggravated sighs at us, and Amanda's nails were starting to grow. Lois slowly sipped just one cup of coffee rather than gulping her usual three. *If only we could stay longer*, I thought to myself.

"What are we going to do today?" Amanda asked as she sliced into a fresh slice of pineapple.

"What would you like to do?" I replied admiring the tropical colors on her fruit plate.

"Do they give tours of the island?" Luke inquired as he forked a homemade waffle with banana into his mouth.

"I can ask Darly. I haven't seen any brochures for something like that." We sat comfortably quiet and pondered until a thought hit me. "You know, last time I was here, I went to a really cool local restaurant on the other side of the island. If it's still there, maybe we could all go for lunch?"

"That sounds like fun," Lois chimed in. "Your father said he should be done with his golf game by one, if you don't mind waiting until then."

An older woman came over to our table carrying a coffee pot. "More coffee for anyone?" she said without a smile. All the adults at our table lifted their cups.

When she reached mine, I asked her, "Do you know if that restaurant on the other side of the island that serves all different types of conch and the best mango coladas is still there?" I pointed directly west.

"You mean Conch Creations?" she cheered up a bit and looked at me surprised.

"Yes, that's it," I said excitedly.

"Ya, that's still there. You been there?" her eyebrows were scrunched.

"Years ago, but I still remember it. The food was delicious and it was nice to experience something more local to the island."

"They open around eleven," she put the coffee pot down on the table and rubbed her arm. "You will need to arrange a taxi to take you over there at the front desk."

"Do you know what time they close for lunch?" I hoped we wouldn't get there too late if we waited for my dad.

"They don't close once they open for the day until everyone go home at night, it's an island, what else is there to do?" she finally smiled.

I smiled back at her and thanked her. She picked her coffee pot up and went to top off the table next to us.

"How about it? Lunch at Conch Creations today?" I

announced to our group.

"Sure why not?" Luke agreed. Lois nodded, Amanda said, "Okay," and Sarah threw in an "All right."

* * *

An old white van with a banged up back fender arrived promptly at 1:30. My dad still had his golf shorts and shirt on. He only changed his hat to one with a larger brim to better cover his balding head. He said under his breath, "Are you sure about this?" to me as everyone else opened a squeaky door and climbed in. The driver, a gentleman who resembled Morgan Freeman, helped Lois in and then reached out for my hand. I leaned back and whispered to my dad, "Just go with it."

The girls dug into the seats looking for seatbelts but didn't find any. I gently reached over to their seat in front of mine and touched their shoulders. They turned around and I mouthed, "Don't worry about it," hoping the driver wouldn't see me.

"Conch Creations, right?" he confirmed as he glanced into the rearview mirror.

"Yes, please," I told him.

Once we were out of the resort and bouncing along the dirt road, our driver started to try and make conversation. "Your first time to the island?" he looked at his rearview mirror again.

Surprisingly, my father who ended up riding shotgun, chimed in probably to help keep the driver focused on the road. "Yes, except for my daughter, who's been here before. That's why we are going to this place; she says it's good."

"Best food on the island." He beamed.

"Will you be able to pick us up?" my father asked a little concerned.

"Oh, yes, man, the bartender, he have my number. Whenever you ready to go, you just tell him to call me."

"Is cab driving your line of work?" my father asked him, somewhat skeptical because it was obvious that not a lot of tourists were being driven around. An occasional old car passed us leaving a wake of dust. I cringed, hoping the driver wouldn't take it as an insult.

"Yes, sir, I drive many of the staff to the resort and back to their homes. I take some people to the airport. I keep busy," he beamed another smile at my dad. "I hope to buy a new van soon, this one have over 200,000 miles on it. It's not easy getting a new car on the island, though. Import tax is crazy, man."

"Yeah, I'm finding that out," my dad's tone easing as he continued dialoguing with our driver, businessman to businessman as the rest of us took in the scenes we passed by. Compared to what I remembered, there actually seemed to be some development on the island. A new strip mall was in place, with a breakfast café, jeweler, and investment office. A retail center with a general store, bank, bookstore and gas station was just past the roundabout. The shanty homes with chickens roaming free around them were still the same as we neared the restaurant. The girls poked at each other as they noticed a donkey walking by itself along the road, as my father shook his head.

When a lone horse walked across the road, we stopped to let it pass.

"Can we ride it?" Sarah asked.

"Maybe you two could. I would surely be the straw that broke the horse's back if I tried," Lois said.

We laughed. It was rather skinny.

As we rounded the final bend to the entrance of Conch Creations my heart warmed with delight. The place looked like it hadn't changed a bit.

Our driver, who we now knew as Ray, jumped out first and began opening the van doors releasing its curious passengers. One by one we gathered at the front of the path lined with shells like Dorothy did as she began her journey down the yellow brick road. My father reached for his wallet first and shooed Luke away as he tried to hand him some money. "Thank you, Ray, we'll give you a call later. You're going to come back for us, right?"

Ray paused at the wad of cash, which I guessed my father made sure it was worth for him to pick us back up. "Yes, sir, you no worry about that! Go have a good time."

Satisfied, my father turned and followed us down the crushed shell path lined with Triton shells. The soulful sounds of Bob Marley filtered through us; the air was still and the white sand led to the calm teal blue sea. We entered the shack where they served food. All of its wooden windows painted in teal blue and sunny yellow were secured open as wide as they could go. We all sat around the table closest to the sea with the best view. A lone pair of local boys sat at a nearby table, finishing up their meal.

We waited a good few minutes wondering if anyone

would be coming to serve us. It was only when the boys got up and brought their plates to the kitchen counter, and one leaned over and said something to no one we could see, that a man sprang into action.

"Sorry to keep you waiting, I did not see you come in," he greeted us as he handed us each a menu. "Welcome, my name is Ranaldo. What will you be drinking today?"

My father shot me a look; I just shrugged my shoulders knowing the food would vindicate me. "I'll have one of your famous mango coladas," I started.

"Ah, good choice," he nodded but didn't write anything down.

"That sounds good to me," Lois added.

"I'll have one of your local beers," Luke requested.

Dad followed with, "make that two."

The girls each ordered a virgin mango colada.

"I guess we're having conch." My father concluded after looking at the menu that offered mainly only conch prepared in several varieties. There was chicken for the landlubbers, but we all enjoyed seafood so we ordered an assortment of conch and a big bowl of fries.

The two young men who just left the restaurant dove into the sea with masks and snorkels on. They swam along the top of the water, then slipped below like seals.

"Are they okay? When are they going to come up?" Sarah asked, concerned.

We watched and watched until eventually one by one they spurted for air like whales as they surfaced, then paddled out further.

"You really should try it, Sarah," Amanda told her sister.

"It's amazing what's under there."

I wanted to concur with Amanda, but held back as I noticed for the first time a look of wonder in Sarah's eyes as she stared out after the boys.

"Here you go." Our waiter served the beers, the sounds of a blender swirled in the distance at the bar. "The mango coladas will be here shortly."

"Are there sharks out there?" Sarah asked Ranaldo.

Ranaldo held the cocktail tray to his chest and looked at Sarah. "The ocean is one big fish bowl, with more life than you can imagine. The sharks are part of that, sure, but we rarely have a bad encounter with them here. See those boys out there?" He looked up and pointed. "They been swimming out in those reefs for years, they go WAY out there, they never had a problem with a shark. You Americans, always askin' about the shark." He looked perplexed.

"*Jaws*," Luke said as he let his beer rest on the table. "There was a movie that came out years ago, called *Jaws*. It was a story about great white shark that ate people. I know when I saw it as a kid, I thought twice about going in the water!"

"Ah, well I can tell you that we don't have any Jaws here that I know of," Ranaldo headed back to the bar when we heard the blender go silent.

"If you're rethinking about giving snorkeling a try, I'll go with you later," Luke offered.

Sarah looked back at the sea and ran her fingers through her straight, silky blown dried hair, "Naa, but thanks, Dad."

"I snorkeled many years ago, in the Bahamas," Lois

announced proudly.

"You never told me that," my dad replied.

"There's a lot of things I haven't told you," she turned and winked at the rest of us. "It really was marvelous, I highly recommend it."

Ranaldo halted the conversation as we watched him balance four mango coladas, overflowing with yellow slush, two with a pineapple slice, the other two with kiwi slices clinging to the edge of the glasses. He served the girls the pineapple ones, then Lois and I the other two. He pulled a dishtowel out of his pocket and wiped the edges. "We want to make sure you get your money's worth here," he joked.

The guys ordered another round of beers and then we raised our glasses for a toast, awkwardly sitting in a moment of silence until someone came up with the perfect thing to say. Luke raised his glass the highest and cheered, "To enjoying paradise together."

The clan followed with, "Cheers!" clanking glasses together and taking a sip of their cocktails.

"This is yummy," Lois wrapped her lips around her straw again and drew in another sip.

"Really yummy." Both girls agreed.

"Would you like to try a sip of mine?" Luke nodded and I handed him my glass. My father reached over to Lois and took a sip of hers.

A rare perfect moment; everyone agreed on something and looked happy. We sat sipping our drinks, watching the boys out at sea, and listened to Lois describe her underwater adventures in the Bahamas. "I once saw a giant sea turtle, I mean giant, as big as a dog gliding through the coral reefs. Fish in every color you can imagine, the blues were so vibrant they glowed."

"Did you see any sharks?" Sarah asked, still not convinced it was safe out there.

"I did, two actually, but they were both nurse sharks sleeping under a big mountain of coral. They were no bother," she waved her hand.

"Okay, you ready for your feast?" Ranaldo announced as he came out of the kitchen door holding a large tray filled with platters of conch and a big bowl of French fries. We all sat up in anticipation. The aroma of the curry wafted over our table, while the round crunchy fried conch fritters steamed. Lois reached first for a helping of ceviche conch, my dad reached for a serving of something I didn't have the last time I was there.

"What's that?" I asked Ranaldo.

"That is our newest creation, Coconut Conch Stew." He stood and watched as my dad took his first bite of it.

"It's delicious," my dad slurped as he dove back into his bowl with his spoon.

Surprisingly, the girls ventured into the unknown dishes with a curiosity they never showed when I cooked something new. "You have to try this one," Amanda told Sarah, while Sarah said, "Try this one."

The conversation came to a standstill. The only sounds were "Mmmm" or "Yumm" from our table. We ate like we just washed ashore after days out at sea until finally our stomachs said, "No more."

"Oh, my God, that was the best meal I have had in a long time," Lois said as she wiped her mouth clean with her napkin, leaned back in her chair and took a sip of her colada until it rumbled with the sound of air.

"Very good," my father said.

"Why didn't you tell us about this place sooner?" Luke complained as he continued to pick at a conch fritter, the bread-like center filled with chunks of conch and herbs.

The girls appeared to be too stuffed to comment.

"I'm glad you liked it," I replied as I pushed my empty plate away.

"You didn't like your meal I see," Ranaldo joked as he cleared away the dishes.

"It was outstanding," my dad applauded.

As Ranaldo stacked the empty plates onto his tray we watched as the boys ventured out from the sea onto the sand. Each of them carried a bag made of netting. They sat on the beach and reached into the bags, inspecting their treasures, one by one.

"What did they find?" Sarah asked.

"Oh, those boys are always finding some kind of new sea creatures. Why don't you go down and look for yourselves."

"Can we?" Amanda asked excitedly as she sat at the edge of her chair.

"Go ahead," I replied and off they jetted down to the beach.

"You ready for our homemade rum cake?" Ranaldo pitched.

"Rum cake? I couldn't eat another thing right now." My dad spoke for all of us.

"How about some rum punch? You can go relax on the

lounge chairs by the bar, they will make you some nice rum punch. Then later when your appetite is back, we'll bring you some rum cake."

We looked at each other, nodded, and headed to lounge on the chairs like overstuffed monk seals. The girls looked like they successfully introduced themselves to the boys, who showed them their catch. A welcome soft breeze began to stir and the palm trees swooshed gently above us. Before we could say no, we each had a pink orange sunset rum punch in our hands and we sipped away blissfully. Jimmy Buffet played, followed by a reggae song I never heard.

The sea is bliss
Like a midnight kiss
There's nothing else like this
Nothing else like this
So put your worries away
Let your hips start to sway
Now let your arms reach out
And dance

I looked over at my dad who was gently tapping his foot, Lois was bobbing her head back and forth, and even Luke was swaying in his chair. Our eyes were glittering.

"That is not how you dance," Ranaldo shouted from the restaurant. "You have to get up from your chairs." He laughed, lifting his hands in the air as he came closer and retrieved me out of my lounge chair.

As the song played, my body grooved. Lois pulled my

dad out of his chair and joined us on the sand dance floor. A female bartender came from behind the bar and convinced Luke to get up and dance. In the haze of the rum, I felt joy, relaxed and free.

We danced, switched partners, and waltzed together in a big circle through several more local songs. Sarah tapped me on my shoulder, "Mom?"

It took a few more taps before I responded to her. "What, honey?"

"Can we go snorkeling with the boys?"

I stopped dancing and looked down at the beach. Amanda was still there holding up a sea critter while the boys explained something to her. I didn't want to interrupt the opportune moment to see Sarah enjoy a bit of raw nature. "Sure, but don't go out too far, you have to stay where we can see you."

She ran back down to the beach shouting, "We can go!"

As the song came to an end, the four of us laughed and heaved ourselves back into our lounge chairs.

"Oh, I haven't had such a good time in a long while." Lois said. My dad reached over and held her hand. Although I wouldn't want to have Lois as my mother, I couldn't help but think that maybe she is more of what my father needed in a wife. Luke scooted his chair closer to mine and wrapped his arm around me. I closed my eyes for a moment and let the delight sink in.

"What are the girls doing?" Luke asked. My eyes followed his pointed finger.

We both watched as they shed their clothes, their bathing suits on underneath. They had decided after day one it was just easier having their bathing suits on all day instead of constantly changing. The boys pulled out snorkels and masks from a storage bin near the restaurant and handed them to the girls. They adjusted the straps until they fit onto their faces. They paired up and walked slowly into the water.

The boys and Amanda dunked under to show Sarah how to leave the snorkel above the water in order to breathe. Hesitant at first, she only allowed the glass of the mask to lie on the water's surface. Then eventually she submerged her head deeper.

"But I told Sarah I'd go snorkeling with her," Luke cried.

I squeezed his hand tight and smiled at him.

He cocked his head towards mine. "I guess it's just good that she's finally trying it."

Amanda and her partner went out further than Sarah and hers. *Wouldn't it be wonderful if Sharky would join them now?* I thought to myself. But, despite being out there for nearly an hour, he didn't come. The four of them climbed out of the sea, pulling the gear off their heads, as the girls chatted away nonstop. The boys pulled towels from their storage bins and handed them to my daughters, while they stood and allowed the seawater to drip from their skin. Then one reached back into their bin and handed each of the girls something. The girls finished drying, handed them back their towels and said what appeared to be goodbye. The boys wrapped the soggy towels around their waists and walked down the beach.

"Look what they gave us." Amanda handed me a small,

empty conch shell as she sat on the edge of my lounge chair.

"Wow, a conch shell," I said as I admired it, then handed it over to Luke.

"I got one too." Sarah held hers up.

"May I see?" Lois asked and held her hand out.

Sarah placed it in her hand and Lois marveled at it. "I've never seen so many shades of pink; it's beautiful."

Sarah beamed as she stood there, her normally pristine hair, starting to curl from the salt drying in it. Her skin glowed as a few freckles dotted her nose from the sun. If only she could see through my eyes how beautiful her natural beauty is.

"After your adventures at sea, you must be hungry for some rum cake," Ranaldo chimed in.

Somehow, we found room for the rum cake before we made our way back to the resort.

Chapter 57

AMANDA

Mom sat next to me with her seat reclined, her eyes closed and a slight smile on her face just like the dolphins have. I leaned over to see Sarah all the way on the other side of the plane looking out the window. Granddad, Lois, and my dad, each of them doing their own thing; reading, flipping through the seat pocket in front of them or just staring ahead. I wish we could do more things like this all together.

I turned and looked out my window. Big puffy white clouds were below us now. I looked for Sharky, or his family, the whole time we flew up until the clouds blocked the view of the ocean. I didn't see him or his family. But I'm happy he has a family to hang out with. Mom says someone told her he might even have kids. Maybe someday I can go back and meet them too.

I'm glad I didn't see one piece of plastic in the ocean around Triton. Those dolphins should be okay.

Chapter 58

JILL

Coming home was like entering another galaxy. Everything was exactly where we left it. The local paper folded on the coffee table, the shades all drawn closed, a pair of sandals Sarah decided at the last minute not to bring sitting on the third step. It smelled a bit musty from being unused for five days. It was unusually quiet without Peaches. A far cry from the bright, shimmering island we left this morning.

"Can I use your bathroom?" Lois begged clenching her legs together.

"Sure, go right ahead," I waved her on.

The girls, Luke and my dad lugged our bags in from the taxi van we shared to get home from the airport. They made two piles: theirs and ours in the living room.

"Why don't I just drive you home?' Luke offered to my dad. "Save on the taxi fare."

I was surprised when my father took the offer. He handed the driver a few bills and sent him on his way.

Just as Luke was closing the front door, Billy's car pulled in the driveway.

"Peaches!" Amanda ran out to greet them. Peaches

lunged out the backdoor and into her arms. Then she dashed in the house and bounced around absorbing all the pats she could get. Her tongue dragged out of the side of her mouth.

As I watched I held my hands on my chest over my heart. It has been a long time since we had a Rockwell moment like this in our family. The phone rang. Luke went to answer it.

"If it is for me, tell them I will call them back, okay?" I asked.

"She was very good," Mindy, Billy's wife, came over to report. "She is so sweet. We let her sleep in our bed, I hope that's all right?"

"You may have created a monster," I jested.

Luke tapped me on my shoulder. "It's for you, it's Samantha."

Samantha was probably the only person in the world I would interrupt this moment for. "I'll take it in the kitchen."

"Hello, Samantha?" I said as I heard Luke hang the phone up in the living room.

"Hi," she said full of excitement. "I have been waiting for you to get back. I just wanted to tell you that the Church Holiday Sale was a HUGE success! We took one hundred and twenty seven orders for dolls! One of the church members knows how to build websites. He is going to set up a retail site for us. I know that's a lot of dolls to make before Christmas, but my mother found some other women who know how to sew. They said they would help."

One hundred and twenty seven dolls at thirty dollars each, we could easily send Samantha on the mission trip and even send another person. "Wow, that's fantastic!"

"I'm so grateful to you, Mrs. Cooper," Samantha added. "I don't know where I would have gotten the money to go."

My throat grew tight. She is grateful to me. How could I ever express in words my gratitude towards her? Finally, after all these years, I felt like I could live in my own skin. Finally, I could forgive myself. Finally, I could let that horrible night go.

"Samantha, it is I who needs to thank you," was all I could come up with.

I wasn't sure if she brushed it off, didn't get it, or was just so excited about the order for the dolls, but she carried on. "We are going to have a meeting tomorrow night at the church to go through the orders. Can you come?"

"Absolutely."

"Great, see you tomorrow." She hung up the phone.

I let the news sink in. I heard laughter coming from the living room.

"Is everything all right?" Luke asked when I returned to his side.

"Yes, unbelievably, so," I filled them in on Samantha's news.

"That's a lot of dolls, Mom," Sarah said. "I can help you if you want."

"I can help you dress them, just don't ask me to sew," Amanda added.

"We won't," Sarah needled her sister in a joking way.

"Hey, I might not be good at sewing, but I am good at ocean things. I'm going to clean up the whole ocean when I get older!"

Godspeed, my child, Godspeed.

Author's Note

In June of 2013 a dolphin was found dead along the Hudson River near Stony Point. Risso dolphins feed on squid and throw up the beaks as part of the digestive process. This dolphin had over one hundred beaks stuck in its stomach due to the plastic bags causing a blockage in the digestive system.

To learn more about this issue and how to help marine animals, please visit:

http://www.nrdc.org/oceans/plastic-ocean/

http://www.plasticpollutioncoalition.org

http://marinedebris.noaa.gov/info/plastic.html

Let's do what we can to help these magnificent animals.

About the Author

Susan Allison-Dean is a nurse who retired from traditional practice in 1999, after working 13 years as a Wound, Ostomy, Continence Clinical Nurse Specialist. She found a second career in gardening after working in a garden center and completing an organic gardening internship at Highgrove Garden in England. She now co-owns Naturescapes with her landscape designer husband, Robert. She has authored several clinical and horticulture articles and was a contributing author to the bestselling book, Touched By A Nurse. She is passionate about the sea and loves exploring tropical islands. She extends this passion by doing volunteer work benefitting dolphins and whales. Sue splits her time between Armonk, New York and Cary, North Carolina, with her husband and English bulldog, Bubba.

Connect with Susan on Goodreads,
Facebook, Twitter or Pinterest.

www.susanallisondean.com

Made in the USA
Charleston, SC
23 November 2014